As they walked, Clint said, "There's something I don't understand here, Katy."

"What is it?"

"Well, the three of you are obviously very capable in your own right. If the three of you are working together, why do you need me?"

"You will understand soon," she said.

"After you tell me who you're after?"

"Yes."

Who the hell carried enough of a price on his head for three women to split the pot—a four-way split if he bought in? It would have to be someone of the status of a Bill Longley or a Doc Holliday—which would explain the money and the need for the Gunsmith. . . .

Don't miss any of the lusty, hard-riding action in the Charter Western series, THE GUNSMITH:

THE GUNSMITH # 1: MACKLIN'S WOMEN
THE GUNSMITH # 2: THE CHINESE GUNMEN
THE GUNSMITH # 3: THE WOMAN HUNT
THE GUNSMITH # 4: THE GUNS OF ABILENE
THE GUNSMITH # 5: THREE GUNS FOR GLORY
THE GUNSMITH # 6: LEADTOWN
THE GUNSMITH # 7: THE LONGHORN WAR
THE GUNSMITH # 8: QUANAH'S REVENGE
THE GUNSMITH # 9: HEAVYWEIGHT GUN
THE GUNSMITH #10: NEW ORLEANS FIRE
THE GUNSMITH #11: ONE-HANDED GUN
THE GUNSMITH #12: THE CANADIAN PAYROLL
THE GUNSMITH #13: DRAW TO AN INSIDE DEATH
THE GUNSMITH #14: DEAD MAN'S HAND
THE GUNSMITH #15: BANDIT GOLD
THE GUNSMITH #16: BUCKSKINS AND SIX-GUNS
THE GUNSMITH #17: SILVER WAR
THE GUNSMITH #18 HIGH NOON AT LANCASTER
THE GUNSMITH #19: BANDIDO BLOOD
THE GUNSMITH #20: THE DODGE CITY GANG
THE GUNSMITH #21: SASQUATCH HUNT
THE GUNSMITH #22: BULLETS AND BALLOTS
THE GUNSMITH #23: THE RIVERBOAT GANG
THE GUNSMITH #24: KILLER GRIZZLY
THE GUNSMITH #25: NORTH OF THE BORDER
THE GUNSMITH #26: EAGLE'S GAP
THE GUNSMITH #27: CHINATOWN HELL
THE GUNSMITH #28: THE PANHANDLE SEARCH
THE GUNSMITH #29: WILDCAT ROUNDUP
THE GUNSMITH #30: THE PONDEROSA WAR
THE GUNSMITH #31: TROUBLE RIDES A FAST HORSE
THE GUNSMITH #32: DYNAMITE JUSTICE
THE GUNSMITH #33: THE POSSE
THE GUNSMITH #34: NIGHT OF THE GILA

And coming next month:
THE GUNSMITH #36: BLACK PEARL SALOON

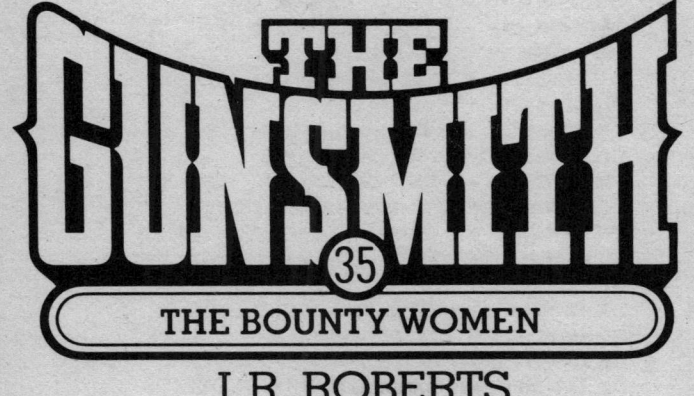

THE BOUNTY WOMEN

J. R. ROBERTS

CHARTER BOOKS, NEW YORK

THE GUNSMITH #35: THE BOUNTY WOMEN

A Charter Book/published by arrangement with
the author

PRINTING HISTORY
Charter Original/December 1984

All rights reserved.
Copyright © 1984 by Robert J. Randisi
This book may not be reproduced in whole
or in part, by mimeograph or any other means,
without permission. For information address:
The Berkley Publishing Group, 200 Madison Avenue,
New York, New York 10016.

ISBN: 0-441-30914-3

Charter Books are published by The Berkley Publishing Group,
200 Madison Avenue, New York, New York 10016.
PRINTED IN THE UNITED STATES OF AMERICA

To "The Campfire"

ONE

The Gunsmith wanted nothing more than to relax, drift and ply his trade as a gunsmith. Over the past few months he'd been involved—unwillingly—in a long hunt for five men wanted for bank robbery and the murder of a child,* and had been recruited—again unwillingly—by the Texas Rangers in a hunt for a Mexican *bandido* chief called Gila.† Now he was tired and only wanted to drift aimlessly and stay out of trouble.

Staying out of trouble was something that a man with a rep could very rarely do—there was always somebody who wanted to test him or make use of him—but he was going to make one hell of a try at it. The only person who would make any use of him over the next few months would be an extremely lovely woman and she—whoever she was—would be able to use him all she wanted—in bed!

The Gunsmith #33: The Posse
†*The Gunsmith #34:* Night of the Gila

Clint Adams was riding slowly through Utah, and the past week had been particularly restful. So far his decision to stay uninvolved had worked like a charm.

The town of Prophecy, Utah, visible from the top of a rise although still a ways off, appeared to be a small, sleepy town, just the kind of place he needed. Fix a few guns, make a few dollars and get some rest.

He stepped down from his rig just long enough to check on Duke, tethered to the rear of the wagon, and make sure he was all right. Discovering a bone bruise late on the big black horse had gotten him into trouble once already,* and he didn't want that to happen again.

"You're in good shape, big boy," he said, patting the horse's huge rump. He was about to climb back aboard the rig when he spotted a rider approaching from behind. Whoever it was could only be heading for Prophecy—or past it—and he decided to wait and see who it was.

It only took a few moments for the rider to get close enough for him to identify her as a woman, and quite a good-looking one at that.

"Hi," she said, reining in by his rig.

"Hello."

She was a slim but shapely redhead, apparently in her late twenties, with the most incredibly sensual face he'd ever seen, even when dust-covered. Her lips were full and her eyes were green, with dark, heavy eyebrows that contributed mightily to the look.

"Heading into Prophecy?" she asked.

"That's right."

"Mind if I ride with you?"

He peered behind her and she laughed and said, "I'm not on the run, if that's what you're worried about."

---

*The Gunsmith #33: The Posse

"Not at all," he said, climbing onto the front seat of the rig. "You're welcome to ride along."

"Thank you."

As they started up she said, "My name's Anne Archer."

"Clint Adams," he said, without bothering to watch her face for a possible reaction. He did, however, notice the tied-down .45 on her hip. A big gun for a woman, and a woman wouldn't be wearing such a weapon unless she was able to handle it. Aside from her obvious beauty, that made her even more interesting to him.

Prophecy might prove to be a pleasant stopover.

"That's a beautiful animal," she said along the way.

"Thank you."

"How long have you had him?"

"Since he was a yearling."

"I guess you're pretty attached to him, huh?"

Remembering the trouble he'd gone through in the past when Duke had been stolen* and once when he had been shot and almost killed,† Clint said, "We've been through a lot together."

The girl was riding a small, surefooted dun, and she patted the horse's neck and said, "That's the way I feel about Skeeter. He's gotten me out of a bad scrape more than once."

"He's a good-looking animal."

"He is, but he's not in a class with yours."

"That's all right," Clint said, looking right at her now. "His rider more than makes up for it."

She smiled and said, "Thanks." When she smiled her

---

*The Gunsmith #28: The Panhandle Search
†The Gunsmith #31: Trouble Rides a Fast Horse

eyes crinkled, and he liked that about her, as he liked everything else he'd seen so far.

When they reached town, they put up their horses at the livery and walked over to Prophecy's small hotel together.

"Doesn't look like this town has a lot to offer," she said idly.

"Oh, I don't know," he replied. He didn't look at her when he said it.

They registered at the hotel, and the clerk mistakenly offered them one room. Clint made sure that he was the one who corrected the man. He was sorry that the town wasn't a little bigger, with more visitors. If there had been only one room left, he could have offered to share it.

"Since we came to town together," she said as they ascended the steps to the next floor, "why don't we meet for a drink after we freshen up?"

"Fine with me."

"I for one could use a bath."

"So could I. I assume that this hotel—if it has a bathtub—has only one. Why don't you go first, and then when I'm finished I'll meet you at the saloon."

"Assuming this town only has one."

"I think that's a safe assumption."

"All right," she said, as they reached her room. "See you in about an hour, then."

She was giving them both one hour to take a bath each. He didn't know many women who could take just their own baths in that little time.

"I'll look forward to it."

"So will I," she said, closing the door between them. He might have been mistaken, but the look on her face seemed to be filled with unspoken promise.

While Clint waited in his room, giving Anne Archer

enough time to take her bath, he kept having mental images of what she must look like getting in and out of the tub. Getting in, her pale skin would be dry, slightly dusty in some areas, but getting out, her body would glisten, her nipples would probably be stiff. What color were her nipples, he wondered. It had been a long time since he'd had erotic thoughts about a woman, this way, and he could feel himself getting very stiff.

He was going to be very disappointed if he was reading Anne Archer's signals wrong.

Ann was already waiting for Clint in the saloon when he got there, with a beer in front of her. There were several other men in the room, all of whom had their eyes on the lovely redhead.

Clint walked to the bar and said, "I'll have a beer, and bring it to the lady's table."

"Might as well forget that, friend," the elderly barkeep advised him.

"Why's that?"

"Every man in this place has already tried, and she's not in the mood."

"Just bring me my beer over there, friend," Clint said, and walked over to Anne's table.

Sitting down, he said, "I understand you've had several offers already."

She laughed and said, "None as good as the first, though."

"The first?"

"Yours."

The bartender came over with the beer, cast an admiring glance Anne's way, and then a look of wonder the Gunsmith's way. What did he have that the other men didn't?

According to the lady, Clint thought, he had the better offer—only he hadn't remembered making one.

Anne Archer had removed her hat for the first time since they'd met, revealing her red hair to be cut short. He liked it, which was no surprise to him. He would have been willing to bet that he could find that this woman had three breasts, and he'd have liked that, too.

She sipped her beer and said, "Oh, that's good." When she very deliberately ran her tongue over her top lip, removing beer suds, the Gunsmith became convinced that she had known who he was before they even spoke. She'd been playing with him since that time, and he was very curious to know why. Obviously they were going to end up in bed, and he didn't mind waiting until then to find the answer.

He sipped his beer, nodded and said, "Cold. Gets rid of whatever dust the bath didn't."

"*That* was heavenly," she said. "There's only one thing that could have made it better."

"I know," he said, deciding to match her boldness with his own. "Company."

She smiled then, slowly and deliberately, still playing him, and said, "You feel it too."

"Yes."

"I halfway expected you to join me in the bath."

"I almost did."

"Almost isn't good enough," she said, running her forefinger around the rim of her beer mug. "We could fix that, you know."

"Now?"

"Now."

"Your room or mine?"

"The closest one to here."

Hers was the first they had come to in the hall at the hotel, which made it the closest.

"Yours, then."

"Let's go."

They got up together, leaving their beers on the table, and left the saloon together.

"What's he got that we ain't got?" one of the men in the saloon asked aloud.

"I don't know," another man replied, "but I say we find out."

TWO

She didn't have three breasts after all, just two, but they were beautiful. They were medium-sized, well-rounded and firm, with pink nipples against very pale skin. There was a sprinkling of freckles in the valley between them, which he explored with his tongue the first chance he had.

"Mmmm," she moaned, cradling his head as he widened his area of exploration to include her breasts and nipples. He sucked on her until her nipples were incredibly hard, and then she pushed his head lower, indicating that she wanted him to explore her charms even further and more fully.

When his nose was nestled in her fragrant bush, she lifted her hips to meet the pressure of his tongue, and he slid his hands beneath her to cup her smooth, firm buttocks. He lingered for a long time, plumbing the sweet depths of her with his mouth, until she was beating the mattress with her fists and closing her thighs around his head.

"Oh, Jesus . . ." she moaned aloud as she came, and

she said, "Quick, Clint, put it in me quickly, before it stops!"

He changed position quickly and drove his rock-hard member into her, prolonging her orgasm. She wrapped her legs around him and began to run that sensuous mouth over his face as he pumped into her. When she wasn't kissing him or licking him, she was murmuring against his face, words that he couldn't quite make out beyond "Oh yes" and an occasional "Damn." Finally she was ready to come again, and she clamped her mouth over his and sucked furiously on his tongue. He felt his own climax building up, and as she bucked wildly beneath him he exploded, spewing his essence into her with incredible force.

"God," she said later, "that was even better than I thought it would be."

"I'll take that as a compliment." He propped himself up on an elbow and began to circle one of her nipples with his forefinger. "Should we get down to business now?"

"Business? What do you mean?" she said, frowning with those marvelous eyebrows.

"Come on, Anne. It's no secret that we've been heading here since before we met."

"Before? How do you figure—"

"I have a reputation for quite a few things, but being stupid isn't one of them. Which rep brought you to me?"

She remained silent for a few moments, and then touched his hand and said, "Okay, you win. I knew you were the Gunsmith all along."

"Well, that's a start."

"Total honesty," she said.

"Strikes me as the best policy."

"A poet too, eh, among your many talents?"

"What are your talents—aside from the obvious, that is?"

She looked at him, the ends of her short hair plastered to her elegant neck by her perspiration.

"I'm a bounty hunter."

"You're a . . . what?"

"I said—"

He laughed and said, "I heard you."

"What's so funny?" she demanded, sitting up.

"Nothing," he said, admiring the line of her back. He put his hand on it and said, "Nothing. What has your profession got to do with me?"

"I'm looking for a man with a big price on his head. I won't tell you his name, or the price, until you've agreed—"

"Agreed to what?"

She looked at him over her shoulder and said, "I'm getting ahead of myself."

"Wait a minute," he said. "You don't want me to help you, do you?"

"Let's say I wouldn't mind."

"No," he said firmly.

"But, Clint—"

"I've been on enough manhunts to last me a lifetime, Anne," he said. "I'm not about to go on another one, and certainly not for a bounty. I'm afraid the answer has to be no."

She studied him that way for a few moments, over her shoulder, and then lay back down beside him and said, "All right."

"That's it? No argument?"

"It was worth asking, but I was prepared for you to say no," she said.

He was impressed with her attitude, although it didn't quite sit right with him.

"What have you got up your sleeve?" he asked.

"Me?" she said, arching her eyebrows over her green

eyes in a display of innocent surprise. "I haven't got any sleeves." And she rolled over so that she was lying on top of him. "Or haven't you noticed?"

She reached between them to guide his rigid penis to her moist portal, and he said, "Yes, I've noticed."

They made love again and then found that they had built up an appetite. They dressed and left her room to go to dinner.

The clerk in the hotel recommended a small cafe at the end of the main street—which would have been little more than an alley in a larger town—and they were walking there when they were suddenly confronted by three men.

"Hello, miss," one of them said. "Finally found somebody to your liking?"

Clint recognized the three of them from the saloon.

"The lady and I are on our way to dinner," he said. "We'd appreciate it if you'd step aside."

"Is that a fact?" the spokesman asked. He was a large man with a full mustache and broad shoulders. "Well, maybe the lady would like some more company for dinner? Like me and my friends?"

"I'd sooner eat with a bunch of cows," Anne said. "Now get out of our way."

"Ooh, she talks tough, don't she, boys?" he asked his friends. Pointing to her gun, he said. "You gonna use that on us, missy? Little heavy for you, isn't it?"

"Not at all," she said. "It fits in my hand real comfortable. I'd be glad to show you, if you like." She moved away from Clint about a foot or so and told the man, "Go ahead, go for your gun."

For a moment the man didn't think she was serious.

"Hey, lady—"

"Mister, either you go for your gun or I'll shoot you like the dog you are."

"Lady, wait a minute—" The man looked at Clint and asked, "Is she serious?"

Clint shrugged and said, "There's only one way to find out, friend."

The man looked about nervously now, seeking help from his friends, but they were backing off steadily.

"We didn't mean no harm," the man said to Clint.

"Tell that to the lady."

"Miss, we was just kidding, you know?"

"Then take a walk."

"Sure," he said. "Sure thing."

The three men quickly crossed the street to get clear of the crazy gal with the big .45. She was too confident for them. She must have known how to use that gun, and they wanted no part of a woman like that.

"Shall we go to dinner?" she asked Clint.

Clint, impressed with her coolness and her refusal to rely on *his* rep to get them out of the situation, said, "By all means—and dinner is on me."

After dinner they went back to Anne Archer's room and made love again, repeatedly. The woman seemed to be suffused with sexual energy, which he swore was transmitted to him. When she was ready for more, so was he, and vice versa. They fit together very well, in bed and out of it, but he had promised himself no involvement, and as much as he liked and enjoyed Anne Archer, he was determined to leave the next morning.

"You're leaving in the morning, aren't you?" she asked him at one point.

"Yes."

"I think I'll stay awhile and rest. I've been hunting for a long time."

"It might be a good idea for you to do that."

"Sure. A little rest and I'll be as good as new."

"You're better than new now, as far as I'm concerned," he said, and they turned toward each other and started all over again.

In the morning they made love again, long and sweetly, and when they were finished she watched him dress.

"I guess we could have saved the expense of the other room," she said, "if I'd spoken up sooner."

"Are you offering to pay for it?"

She laughed and said, "No."

He strapped on his gun and moved toward the bed again. She sat up and he kissed her full lips.

"You are probably the most extraordinary-looking woman I've ever seen," he told her.

"You're sweet," she said, cupping his chin and kissing him again.

"Good-bye, Anne. I'm sorry I couldn't help you."

"I'll miss you, Clint."

"We'll see each other again."

"Yes," she said with an enigmatic smile. "We will, Clint. Good-bye—for now."

THREE

It was several days later when Clint Adams came to the town of Jericho, and Anne Archer was still on his mind. What he needed, he knew, was another woman to divert his thoughts from the lovely, sensuous redhead.

Jericho was a larger town—by far—than Prophecy had been, yet in actuality it was not what one would call a big town. Still, it had more than one livery, more than one hotel, and many more than one saloon. Perhaps he'd stay in Jericho for a few days, play some cards, drum up some business and find another girl to dally with.

He registered at one of Jericho's hotels, took a hot bath, found a good meal—in the hotel dining room—and then made the rounds of the saloons until he found one to his liking.

The Jericho Saloon was the largest the town had to offer, and it in turn offered entertainment in several different forms: liquor, gambling . . . and women.

The women were professionals, which meant that they didn't interest the Gunsmith beyond admiring them from afar. He decided to do some gambling, but not at any of the house-run tables. There were a couple of independent poker games going on, and he ordered a beer and settled down to wait for an empty seat to present itself.

A player at one of the tables caught his eye, and he watched with interest. It was a woman, a tall, full-bodied, brassy blonde who seemed to be holding her own with the men at the table, and more. She was having a good time, laughing boisterously whenever she raked in her chips—which was often—and a couple of the men at the table didn't seem to appreciate that.

Finally, while she was pulling in a particularly large pile of chips, the men could take no more. It was apparently embarrassing to them to be beaten by a woman.

"Listen, lady, would you mind not laughing so hard when you take a pot? It ain't nice," one of the men said. He was a particularly large specimen with bulky shoulders, bulging arms and a large paunch.

"Nice? Friend, if you were looking for a nice game, you picked the wrong table," she told him in an overly loud voice. "I sat down here to win some money, and if most of it happens to be yours, that's your hard luck."

"Listen, bitch—" the man said from between clenched teeth, but she didn't give him much of a chance to continue. She was obviously used to handling men like him.

"Mister, if you're gonna talk that way to me, you're gonna get me mad. If I get mad, you ain't gonna like it."

"What do you think you're gonna do?" the man demanded.

"I don't think you want to know," she said, calling for the cards since the next deal was hers.

"I wanna know!"

"All I want to know is, should I deal you in or out?"

"Don't deal at all," the man said, slamming a meaty

THE BOUNTY WOMEN

hand down on the table. "We got something to settle."

The woman gave him a look of exasperation and put the deck of cards down on the table.

"Mister, what's your name?"

"Wilson. Why?"

"I like to know man's name before I embarrass him in front of a roomful of men."

Wilson laughed and said, *"You're* gonna embarrass *me?* Lady, I'm gonna pull off your clothes in front of all these men and give you a nice friendly poke right here on this table—and you're gonna love it."

"A nice friendly poke?" she asked, eyeing him skeptically. "With what? I'd be willing to put money on the table that you ain't got much more than a . . . a worm, wiggling at the end of a fishhook."

The men at the table, and several men at surrounding tables, found that funny and laughed aloud so that the big man's face suddenly turned beet-red.

"Bitch!" he shouted, jumping to his feet and almost overturning the table. It was the blonde who kept it from falling by slapping her hands down on it to steady it. "Get ready to be mounted and rode out hard!"

She stood up, and Clint could see the tied-down .44 on her generous hip. She measured easily six feet tall, and had the full breasts that a woman her height should have.

"Come ahead, friend," she said to Wilson.

The big man moved around the table and closed on the woman, and Clint, who would ordinarily have stepped in, was interested in what the woman's reaction would be.

She moved away from the table as the man charged her, and then suddenly sidestepped, sticking her foot in his path. He tripped on it and went sprawling across another table, which collapsed beneath his weight.

"I'm over here," she called out to him.

He turned and clambered to his feet, his eyes burning with hatred now. He ignored the gun on his hip, wanting only to get his hands on her, and the woman likewise paid no attention to her gun.

He closed on her again, and this time, incredibly, she stood her ground and shot her right arm straight out, catching him beneath the chin with the heel of her hand. It stopped him cold, staggering him and sending him back a few steps until he tripped on the debris of the broken table and fell on his ass on the floor. He sat there for a moment, shaking his head like a wounded bull to clear it, and then slowly got to his feet. The laughter going on around him fueled his hatred, and suddenly he shouted, "All right, grab her!"

It became apparent then that he had a few friends in the place because two men stepped forward and took hold of the girl's arms.

"Now I'm gonna mount you, girl," Wilson said. "Take her down!"

That was when the Gunsmith stepped in.

He moved forward, pushing through the onlookers, and swung a right that caught one of her captors beneath his left ear. The man went down like a sack of feed.

Another man stepped out from the crowd and swung at Clint, who ducked beneath the blow and brought his knee up into the man's midsection. The girl, meanwhile, had turned to the other man who was holding her and simply hit him on the jaw with her right fist, dropping him. She then turned to face Wilson again, who had decided that it was time for his gun.

"Don't," she cautioned him, but the warning was futile. He was too incensed to hear her, and he was also overly anxious to remove his gun from his holster. His fingers closed on the butt of his pistol, then groped for a proper hold on it to draw it. By that time the woman had coolly drawn her own gun and fired one shot, which caught him in one meaty shoulder.

The other men began to stagger to their feet, but Clint moved in next to the woman and said to them, "Take it easy. It's all over."

He had not drawn his gun, but his manner persuaded the men that the incident was indeed finished.

"Help your friend. He's going to need a doctor."

As they moved forward to assist their pal, the woman looked at Clint and said, "Thanks for the help."

"My pleasure."

"My name's Sandy Spillane."

"Clint Adams."

"Can I buy you a drink?"

"Sure," he said. And then, as he spotted a man with a badge working his way across the room, he added, "After we talk to the law."

"You're on."

FOUR

Thanks to a roomful of witnesses, it didn't take very long for Clint and Sandy to tell their story to the local sheriff's satisfaction. It also helped that the lawman knew who Clint was, and was impressed.

"Shall we have that drink in a different saloon?" Sandy suggested after they left the sheriff's office.

"Sure," Clint said. "In a quieter one."

They found another, considerably smaller saloon with fewer people, and installed themselves at a corner table.

"Not many men would take a hand in somebody else's troubles," she commented.

"I know," Clint said. "I'm trying to break myself of the habit."

"Well, I'm glad for my sake that you haven't broken it yet," she said, smiling.

Walking side by side with her, Clint found that Sandy Spillane, in her boots, was about an inch taller than he was, which he really didn't mind much. Once he got her boots off—and he *was* looking forward to that—he was sure she'd be an inch or so shorter than he, but a woman's height really didn't matter to him. They were all the same height, lying down.

Up close, he could see that Sandy was probably in her early thirties, with shoulder-length, wheat-colored hair and blue eyes. She had full lips and a firm jaw and was, facially, a very handsome woman. Her body was very full, with large round breasts, and hips to match.

"You didn't look to be doing too badly for yourself," he said. "You handle yourself—and your gun—pretty well."

"Thanks. Coming from you, that's a great compliment."

That meant she knew who he was, even though the sheriff had never once called him the Gunsmith.

"Yes, I know who you are," she said, reading his look. "I recognized your name."

"Then you know more than I know, and that's not fair," he said. "Tell me about yourself."

"I don't mind talking about myself," she said with an odd look on her face; on another woman he would have called it coy, but she wasn't the type. "But not here," she amended.

"Where, then?"

She looked him in the eye and said, "I'm a very outspoken lady, Clint. In fact, there are some people who would say I'm not even a lady."

"They're wrong."

"Thanks, but that remark just makes me want to stick to my decision."

"You've made a decision?"

"Yes," she said, leaning her elbows on the table. "I've decided to go to bed with you tonight."

"Is that so?"

THE BOUNTY WOMEN

"If you want me, that is, because I certainly want you. If that's too bold for you, just let me know."

"Why don't we go up to my room and we can discuss it?"

She smiled broadly and said, "I thought you'd never ask."

Sandy Spillane had possibly the largest, firmest breasts Clint had ever had the pleasure of running his mouth and tongue over.

As soon as they had entered the room, Sandy was all over him, undressing him and pulling her own clothing off. When she took off her boots, Clint found that he'd been right—she was almost two inches shorter than he was.

"Oh God, I've been wanting this," she said, taking hold of his stiff shaft and leading him to the bed by tugging at it.

When they got close to the bed, he pushed her down on it and then began exploring her breasts with his mouth.

"Are they too big?" she asked.

"No," he said, "they're perfect." He took a perfect pink nipple between his teeth and worried it there, causing her to gasp and clasp his head close to her.

He wasn't lying. Her breasts were perfect for her, just as Anne Archer's had been perfect for *her*. Clint was surprised that even while in bed with Sandy Spillane, who was a lot of woman in more ways than one, he was still thinking of Anne.

He decided to apply himself totally to the woman who was now in bed with him, and to that end he began to run his mouth down over her ribcage, then her slightly convex belly, until he reached the blonde forest between her legs.

As a young man, Clint had never done this sort of thing

much, but he noticed that much more of late he'd been doing it with most of the women he bedded. He found that he enjoyed it immensely. He enjoyed the smell and the taste of a woman, and he relished the powerful feeling it gave him. When a woman's belly began to tremble—the way Sandy's was now, as he lashed her with his tongue— signaling her approaching climax, he knew that he had her right where he wanted her. He knew that he was giving her intense pleasure, which was an important part of sex for him. At times his bed partner's pleasure was even more important to him than his own. Usually he made damn sure that his women had all they could handle before he allowed himself to achieve completion.

Sandy's heavy thighs came up and closed around his head as she began to come, and he reached up and palmed her breasts, tweaking her nipples to intensify her pleasure.

"Oh Lord, I want you in me, Clint," she said then, spreading her legs to release him. "Put it in me, please do . . ."

He took that as an order and obeyed immediately. Sandy seemed to be as deep inside as she was big outside. As he plunged into her—and she was so wet and slick that it was like plunging into a small lake—he cupped her big buttocks and pulled her to him to achieve maximum penetration.

"Oh yes, damn you, yes . . ." she moaned, rolling her head back and forth on the pillow. This time her powerful legs came up and surrounded his waist, and he could feel the strength she had there.

The bed was creaking and squeaking now, as their combined weight made it protest loudly. She was bouncing her hips up and down with increasing speed, actually lifting him off the bed with her each time. She was a big, strong girl, and Clint found that riding her was like riding an unbroken filly.

Finally her insides yanked his orgasm from him forcefully, and he emptied himself into her while she moaned and cried beneath him. The sensation of him filling her added to the pleasure she was receiving from her own climax.

"God . . ." she said, and Clint wondered for the thousandth time what made women call to their deity—whoever it happened to be—or curse during sex. Some women did one or the other, and others—like Sandy—did both. Very rarely did he come across a woman who could wordlessly enjoy sex, but he guessed that was something inherent in women.

"Time for that talk," he said, after they had caught their breaths.

"About me?"

"Yup."

"I'll bet you can't guess what I do."

"For a living," he asked, "or for pleasure?"

"You *know* what I do for pleasure."

"You're a schoolteacher."

She laughed and asked, "Do I *look* like a schoolmarm?"

"No, ma'am," he said, "you look more like a—" He stopped short, because he couldn't believe what he'd been about to say. He must have subconsciously been thinking about Anne Archer again.

"What?" Sandy asked, prompting him. "What were you going to say?"

He decided to tell her.

"I was going to say that you look like a bounty hunter."

She stared at him in surprise and said, "Now how did you know that?"

It was his turn to stare at her. Prior to entering Utah a week ago, he had only met one female bounty hunter in his life, and that was Lacy Blake,* and he'd been tremendously impressed with her. Now, within a week, he had met *two* more—both of whom had impressed him in more ways than one.

"What's wrong?" she asked.

"I'm just surprised, that's all," he said. "I was only kidding."

"Well, you were right on the money. In fact, I'm on the hunt right now."

"Is that a fact?"

She sat up suddenly, her large breasts standing out impressively from her chest without the hint of a sag.

"Say, maybe you'd like to hook up with me. There's a lot of money involved."

Clint was starting to wonder how much of a coincidence a coincidence could be. *Two* lady bounty hunters trying to get him to join them?

"How much?"

She narrowed her eyes and said, "I don't think I'll tell you that unless you agree to help me."

"Well, who are you after?"

"I can't tell you that, either."

"Well, it really doesn't make much of a difference," Clint said. "I'm not interested in hunting men for money."

Looking as if she'd been stung by his words, she asked, "Do you see something immoral about it?"

"That's not what I meant," he said, putting his hand on

The Gunsmith #24: Killer Grizzly

her smooth shoulder. "It's just that I've done enough of that in my life."

"I see."

"Come here," he said. He pulled her down to him, and she twisted so that her breasts were pressed against his chest. He kissed her, gently at first and then with increasing vigor until their tongues were dueling.

"I'm sorry," he said.

"That's okay," she assured him. "I'm used to doing *some* things alone, anyway."

"Well," he said, moving one hand down the line of her spine until he reached the indentation between her buttocks, "I'm glad it's only *some* things."

In the morning, Clint and Sandy had breakfast together and discussed their immediate futures. Sandy said she was leaving town to continue her hunt, and if she was leaving town, there was nothing there to keep the Gunsmith around.

Clint walked Sandy to the livery and allowed her to leave town ahead of him. He wanted to check over his rig before continuing on.

"I'm sorry I couldn't help you," he said, echoing the words and sentiment he had used with Anne Archer.

"That's all right, Clint," she said. "I'm just real glad I'm an outspoken, bold hussy and that we had last night."

"So am I."

She moved close to him, kissed him tenderly and said, "Good-bye, Clint Adams. We'll see each other again, real soon."

Sandy had already left and Clint was underneath his rig, checking his axles, when he realized that Anne Archer had said the same thing.

FIVE

The more he thought about it over the next day or so, the more convinced Clint became that he should have asked Sandy if she knew Anne. Perhaps the big payday both women were pursuing was on the head of the same man. The two women might have been able to join forces and work together—if indeed they were not already doing just that.

Never a big believer in coincidences, Clint realized that it was just possible that both women could have been working together to try to get him to help them with their hunt.

There were a couple of ways of looking at this. The first was that they would have had to know he was in Utah to set themselves up the way they did, in consecutive towns, to work their way into his acquaintance—if not his bed—before springing it on him that they were bounty hunters. Could they have seen him, recognized him, and planned that far in advance? He didn't think it was too likely.

The other possibility was that there might be a flyer out

on somebody big, of late, that would bring bounty hunters out of the woodwork. Since he was no longer a lawman, he no longer kept up on current wanted posters.

Of course, he had been equally impressed with the way the two women had handled themselves—in all ways—and they could very well have been competent bounty hunters simply working the same area.

Still, the Gunsmith hated coincidences almost as much as he hated being called the Gunsmith.

The next town was called Jory, and as size went, it was somewhere between Prophecy and Jericho. Having been preoccupied in the last two towns with Anne and Sandy—and since the odds were against his finding another such exceptional woman in a third consecutive town—he figured on actively plying his trade here.

When he pulled into the livery and made arrangements for his animals, he asked the liveryman if there was a gun shop in town.

"No sir," the man answered. Actually, at seventeen or eighteen he was more boy than man.

"Where do people get their guns repaired?"

"Ain't much use for a gun in this town, mister, but when something does go wrong, people generally try to fix it themselves."

That meant some people would have been successful and some wouldn't have been. There might be some malfunctioning guns sitting around waiting to be fixed, so Clint told the kid—whose name was Claude—to let everyone know that he was open for business.

"Yessir, I sure will. Fact is, I got me a squirrel gun could use some lookin' at."

"Bring it around, Claude, and I'll take care of it for you free of charge."

"Thank you."

That was called casting bread upon the waters, and Clint was hoping that it would indeed come back in big loaves.

He got directions to the Jory Hotel—one of two hotels in town—removed his rifle and saddlebags from his saddle, and went to get himself a room.

Jory looked like a pleasant little town, and Clint thought he might stay a while. He might have stayed longer in Jericho except for the incident in the saloon and the fact that the sheriff knew who he was.

Of late, in an attempt to retain some semblance of anonymity, short of lying about his name, Clint had not even been checking in with the local lawmen in towns he'd passed through.

He registered in a room, paid extra for a bath and, after the bath, went in search of lunch. The drill had been the same in both of the towns he'd stopped in so far in Utah. Of course, the last two stops had been real pleasant—thanks to Anne and Sandy—but the stop in Jory might, with a little luck, turn out to be profitable.

Not that the Gunsmith was low on funds. He was a partner in a saloon business in Brightwater, Arizona, with a man named Buckskin Frank Leslie,* the profits of which were simply wired to his bank in Labyrinth, Texas. Labyrinth had become something of an unofficial headquarters for Clint. It was where he banked, and kept a mail drop. Still, in spite of that, he enjoyed earning money at his "new" chosen profession.

Clint found a saloon that served food, and enjoyed a simple meat-and-potatoes lunch, accompanied by a cold beer. As he was finishing up, he saw the liveryman,

---

The Gunsmith #16: Buckskins and Six-Guns

Claude, enter carrying an aged, small-caliber Henry rifle that had seen much better days.

"Hope I ain't botherin' you none."

"Not at all. I've finished my lunch."

Claude held the rifle out to Clint and said, "Don't always fire when I pull the trigger."

Clint suspected that among other things the weapon had a faulty firing pin. He examined the piece and found that to be the case.

"I'll take it over to my wagon now, Claude, and fix it up for you. I'll also give it a good cleaning and then I'll show you how to do the same thing. No reason this gun shouldn't shoot a lot more squirrels for you."

"And some rabbits," Claude said excitedly. Apparently the boy liked to hunt.

"And some rabbits."

Clint stood up and they walked back to the livery together. He found out that Claude was actually all of nineteen, and had come into the livery stable when his father died the year before.

"It was his, so now it's mine."

"That's the way it should be."

When they reached the livery, Claude said he had some work to do and Clint climbed into the back of his wagon and got to work on the badly abused but salvageable gun.

He replaced the firing pin and thoroughly cleaned the gun, stopping on a couple of occasions when townspeople knocked on the side of the wagon, inquiring as to whether he had time to work on their guns. He had laid aside the Henry and picked up an equally abused Colt handgun when there was another knock on the side panel of the hardwood wagon. The wagon had once belonged to a peddler, and when the man was killed and his wagon became available at auction, that as much as anything else had been the final impetus for the Gunsmith's decision to give up his badge, buy the wagon and start operating as a traveling gunsmith.

Clint moved to the rear of the wagon to see who was knocking, and was surprised to find a stunning, dark-skinned, dark-haired girl who appeared to be at least part Indian.

"Hello," he said.

"You the gunsmith?" she asked, and it took him a few moments to realize that she was asking him if he was *a* gunsmith and not *the* gunsmith.

"That's right."

She took her gun out of her holster, and he saw that it was a shotgun with the single barrel and stock both cut down to make it a weapon that could be fired one-handed.

"Needs a new firing pin, I think," the girl said. Her hat was off, hanging behind her by a leather thong around her neck, and she swept her hair back away from her face with a practiced jerk of her head.

He cocked the hammer on the gun and saw that it did indeed need a new firing pin. The one it had now had somehow gotten itself bent—almost as if somebody had meant to bend it.

"I can take care of that for you, Miss—"

"Katy Little Flower," she said, staring at him boldly with wide brown eyes. "My mother was full-blooded Comanche."

"And your father?"

She made a face and said, "My mother was never sure."

He nodded, not knowing how to react or reply to the statement.

"When can I come back for it?"

"About an hour, I guess. I've got some other work."

"That's okay," she said. "I'll see you in an hour."

She bent and picked up a rifle she had leaned against the wagon, and he suspected that she was the kind of woman who did not like to be without a gun. She was about five-eight—tall for a woman, but not as tall as Sandy Spillane had been—with full breasts and long legs. Her outfit was buckskin and looked handmade. She was wearing moccasins.

There was a pinto in a rear stall that Clint had been admiring earlier, and now he said, "Is that your horse?"

She turned to look at the horse in question, and then looked back at him and nodded.

"Fine animal."

"Thank you. I will see you in an hour."

"Sure."

He stepped down from the wagon to watch her walk away. She had a no-nonsense kind of walk, light on her feet and very feminine—or perhaps *feline* would have been a better word. She walked and moved the way a cougar would, careful but coiled.

An exceptional-looking woman, he thought, realizing that he was staring at another coincidence. He didn't like it.

SIX

Clint got some more business after Katy Little Flower left, but he made sure he had her gun ready well ahead of the promised time.

Not only was he bothered by her appearance simply because it meant that he'd met three exceptionally desirable women in three consecutive towns in Utah, of all places, but also because she seemed to be the same *type* of woman as the other two. Self-sufficient, independent, confident—and dangerous.

Could she be a bounty hunter as well? There was only one way to find out, and that was to wait for her to come back and then ask her.

A couple of men came by for their weapons and paid Clint before Katy Little Flower finally returned.

He handed her the gun and she accepted it and slid it into her holster—which covered practically her whole thigh—without so much as checking it.

"Aren't you going to check it?"

"I'm sure it's all right."

"Why are you so sure?"

"Because you're—" she started, and then stopped suddenly.

"Because I'm what?"

"Because you're the Gunsmith," she said, and this time it was immediately clear what she meant.

He stepped down from his wagon and said, "I think we should talk."

"I think so too," she agreed.

"Any place in particular?"

"My room," she said, "if you have no objection."

"I have no objection—if you'll feel safe."

She didn't smile when she said, "I'll feel safe."

"All right."

He turned, closed the door to his wagon and locked it.

"Let's go."

She was staying on the second floor of the other hotel that the town of Jory had to offer, in a room that overlooked the street. When she unlocked the door and entered, he stepped inside and waited for her to shut the door behind them before he spoke.

"You bent that firing pin, didn't you?"

"Yes."

"Why?"

"So I'd have an excuse to meet you."

"Why?"

"I've heard a lot about you."

"From whom?"

"My friends."

"Who?"

"Before I go into that, I would like to be honest with you."

That was a switch.

THE BOUNTY WOMEN

"Go ahead," he said, leaning against the wall and folding his arms across his chest.

"I'm a bounty hunter."

"That's a surprise."

She frowned and forged ahead.

"I'd like to ask you for your help. I'm tracking a particularly dangerous man, and I'm not afraid to admit that I could use a man like you on my side."

"I feel I should be honest, as well."

"Yes?"

He pushed himself away from the wall without unfolding his arms, and said, "I've already told your two friends no. You girls have some act."

"I was against it," she said, "from the start."

"Why? And why didn't *you* wait until we were in bed to spring this on me?"

"Because," she said, undoing her gunbelt and removing it, "I'm too honest, I guess. I wanted to get the truth out of the way first."

"First?"

She nodded and hung her gunbelt on the bedpost, then walked up to him.

"Yes. Now that the truth is out of the way, we can go to bed without lies between us. It is the way it should be."

She was serious, and he found himself admiring her for it. She was being honest not only with him, but with herself as well. She wanted to go to bed with him and had decided to remove anything that might taint the act.

"All right," he said. He put his arms around her waist, and she raised her head so he could kiss her. She was tentative at first, but he had the same impression now that he'd had while watching her walk away from him earlier in the day. She was coiled inside, as though set to spring at any moment. He pulled her closer still, and her arms went around him, and she opened her mouth to him fully.

After the kiss, they undressed each other slowly, gently, and he was watching her closely, waiting for her to let go. It was not until they were in bed together, naked and pressed together, that she finally did—and it was worth waiting for.

She went for him with her hands and mouth right away. She cupped his heavy sack in her hands and slid his hard manhood into her mouth slowly, eyes open and watching it disappear inch by inch. When she had as much in her mouth as she could take, she closed her eyes and slid one hand to the base of his shaft, holding it there while she sucked on it eagerly.

He doubted that she had learned this in an Indian camp, and surmised that she had been with a few white men before during her twenty-odd years. She was younger than her two friends, but no less talented in any area.

When he felt that he could take no more without exploding, he reached for her and drew her up to him until she was lying on him fully. She reached between them for his rigid column of flesh and guided it to the moist lips of her sheath. She sighed and closed her eyes as he entered her, and when he was in her fully, she . . . uncoiled!

She went wild, sat up on him and began to ride him forcefully. Her pelvis jarred against his each time she sat back down on him, and she finally braced her hands against his chest and ground herself against him, mouth open and slack, as she came violently. Her entire body trembled and then he was erupting inside of her like a miniature volcano and she was riding him again, reaching for every bit of sensation that she could derive from their time together.

THE BOUNTY WOMEN

Later, lying on top of him, she murmured against his neck, "It was better this way."

"Yes."

"To be honest."

"Yes," he said, although he was by no means saying that it was better with her than it had been with Anne and Sandy. It had been *different* with her, but that did not mean it had been any better or worse.

He knew that he should feel used, now that he knew that all three of them were working together, but he didn't. What he felt was amusement. He realized that they must have recognized him in a place called Tannerville, the first town he had entered in Utah. They had each chosen a town where they would wait for him to arrive and make their offer.

Katy Little Flower assured him that she had gone to bed with him out of an instantaneous attraction to him, and added that she felt sure it was the case with the others as well.

"We never once planned to sleep with you to try to get you to come with us."

"Where are Anne and Sandy now?" he asked.

"They will be here tomorrow."

"Then we'll all talk."

"Is there a chance—?"

"Tomorrow, Katy," he said, rubbing his palms over her slim buttocks.

She picked up her head to look at his face, and smiled for the first time since they'd met.

"I am more concerned with right now," she said.

"I couldn't agree more."

SEVEN

They had dinner together and then went their separate ways, to demonstrate to each other that a roll in the hay didn't join them at the hip. Clint still had some work to do, and Katy had things to do as well.

They did meet later on and retired to Katy's room once again, where they spent the night together.

"What happens in the morning," he asked at one point, "when your girlfriends get here? I've been to bed with all of you, which is, I guess, no secret."

"No, but come tomorrow we shall have to revert to a business relationship."

"That is, if we're to be doing any business," he reminded her.

"Yes," she said, and they discussed it no further.

In a larger town the arrival of Anne Archer and Sandy Spillane riding down the main street together would have attracted a lot of attention. In Jory a few heads turned, but there weren't enough people on the street to make their arrival an event.

As they reined in their horses in front of Katy Little Flower's hotel, she bounded off the boardwalk to meet them. Clint was sitting in a straight-backed chair on the front porch of his hotel, and to him those three women together at the same time—hell, in the same state—was indeed an event to be remembered.

All three girls looked over at Clint, and then Katy started toward him while the other two girls went to put their horses up at the livery.

"They will meet us at the saloon after they've taken care of their horses," she told him.

"Fine," he said, stepping down into the street. "Shall we go?"

As they walked, Clint said, "There's something I don't understand here, Katy."

"What is it?"

"Well, the three of you are obviously very capable in your own right. If the three of you are working together, why do you need me?"

"You will understand soon," she said.

"After you tell me who you're after?"

"Yes."

Who the hell carried enough of a price on his head for three women to split the pot—a four-way split if he bought in? It would have to be someone of the status of a Bill Longley or a Doc Holliday—which would explain the money and the need for the Gunsmith. As competent as these girls were, they were not in the same league with those men.

When they reached the saloon, they staked out a back table and ordered four beers. A few moments later, Katy's two partners walked in.

Clint had some momentary apprehension about sitting at the same table with three women, all of whom he had bedded, but he disregarded those feelings when he realized that all three of these women were professionals.

At least he hoped they were.

"Hello, Clint," Anne said, casting a warm look his way. Sandy smiled and nodded to him as she sat.

With all three women in the same place at the same time, Clint found his eyes resting on Anne Archer more often than on the others. Physically, she was easily the loveliest, especially with that sensuous face.

"I've got one question for the three of you before you start any explanations."

"What is it?" Anne said. Clint had the immediate impression that she was the spokeswoman, in spite of Sandy's brashness.

"How long have you all been doing this?"

"We're all pros, if that's your question," Sandy said.

"That was it."

"Sandy's been at it five years," Anne said, "Katy and I started three years ago."

"Working together?"

"We've all worked together from time to time, but it's not a permanent partnership."

"I see. Only when the price is big enough?"

"And the risk," Anne said.

"Like now?"

"Yes."

"All right," he said, sitting back, "I'm ready for your pitch."

The three women exchanged glances and then Anne shrugged and said, "No pitch, really. The man we're after has a big reputation, and a well-deserved one. Two of us have seen him in action. That's Sandy and myself."

"Who is he?"

They exchanged glances again and then Anne said, "Bill Wallmann."

"What?"

"Wallmann," Sandy said. "The price is five thousand, dead or alive."

"Five thousand?" Clint asked in surprise.

He knew Wallmann, of course. He had run into him several times, most recently in the Dakotas.*

"Dead or alive? I don't understand. Wallmann works for hire, he's not an indiscriminate killer."

"Maybe he never used to be," Anne said, "but he is now."

She took a folded piece of paper out of her pocket and opened it up, smoothing it out on the table. It was a wanted poster, and she passed it to Clint. The illustration was indeed a rough portrait of Bill Wallmann, and according to the poster he was wanted for five murders in three states.

"The story goes that he instigated the gunfight in each case, antagonizing men he knew were no match for him, making it impossible for them to back down and maintain their self-respect and manhood."

"I find this very hard to believe. I know Wallmann—"

"You *knew* him," Sandy said, tapping the poster. "Nobody knows *this* Bill Wallmann."

There was sadness in her voice as she spoke, and Clint wondered about the source.

"He's changed, Clint," Anne said, breaking into his thoughts. "Drastically."

"I'd have to talk to him to believe that."

"Then you'll join us?"

The Gunsmith #30: The Ponderosa War

"I didn't say that."

"But you just said—"

"I'd said I'd have to talk to Wallmann before I believed this," he said, touching the poster, "but that doesn't mean I'm going to hunt him down. I've told each of you that I'm tired of that. I've done enough of it."

There was a long silence, and then Sandy slapped her hand down on the poster and said, "Well, I guess that's that."

"We have to respect your feelings," Anne said to Clint, but he had the feeling she was talking more to herself and the other two women.

"What will you do now?" he asked.

"That's easy," Sandy said, folding the poster up and passing it back to Anne.

"We'll go after him," Katy Little Flower said.

"Five thousand, split three ways," Anne said. "That's too good to pass up, Clint."

Pursuing his earlier thoughts, Clint realized Wallmann was in a class with Longley and Holliday, which meant that these three women were not in Wallmann's class at all. Still, maybe together they stood a chance . . .

"I can only wish you luck, then."

Anne smiled at him and stood up.

"Don't feel guilty, Clint. We took a shot, and you have every right to turn us down."

For a moment Clint and Anne locked gazes, but then the other two girls stood up as well, and Clint averted his gaze. He wished that he and Anne could speak to each other alone, but he couldn't very well arrange that in front of the other two.

"We'll be leaving tomorrow morning," Anne said. "Will you be around to say good-bye?"

Clint was very careful to look at all three of them as he said, "I'll be around."

Having Anne Archer in the same town with him, and knowing that he couldn't touch her, played on Clint's mind for the remainder of the day. Also, her last remark about not feeling guilty had been right on the money. He knew that if anything happened to any of those girls he would feel guilty, but he kept telling himself that they were pros and knew what they were doing. They knew the risks they were taking by going after a man like Bill Wallmann.

He worked on some guns the rest of the day, then went to the saloon in search of some distraction. There were a couple of girls working the place, but none of them could hold a candle to the three female bounty hunters that were occupying his mind. Instead he found a poker game and played until his eyes started to droop, then went back to his hotel room.

He was just drifting off to sleep when there was a soft knock on his door. It could only be one of the women, but which one?

He got up from the bed, made a mental bet with himself on which one it was, and opened the door.

"Hi," Anne Archer said.

He won the bet.

EIGHT

"May I come in?"

"Should we expect any more company?"

She grinned and said, "No," and he didn't ask her how she could be so sure.

"Come on in."

"Have you come to make a last-ditch pitch?"

"No," she said. "I just came to be with you—if you don't mind."

"*I* don't mind, as long as your friends don't."

She stepped close to him, put her arms around his neck and said, "They don't."

Anne was the smallest of the three girls—Sandy being close to six feet, Katy Little Flower about five-eight, and Anne more like five-five—but she seemed to fit very well in the circle of Clint's arms.

He kissed her and she opened her mouth with unrestrained eagerness. He picked her up, carried her to the bed and undressed her, then knelt by the bed and began to explore her body with his mouth. When she couldn't take any more of that, she literally pulled him onto the bed with her and then climbed on top of him, guiding his throbbing organ inside her. It was over very quickly, and then she was lying beside him.

"You were like a starving woman," he said.

"I have been starving ever since we were together," she said. "I never met a man like you before. You're special."

"I hope this isn't leading up to—"

She slapped his flat stomach with her hand, hard enough to sting, and said, "It's not leading up to another pitch for you to go after Wallmann with us, or anything else. I'm just telling you how I feel."

"Okay, I'm sorry."

"How do *you* feel?"

"I like you, Anne, very much."

"All right," she said. "Let's not go any further than that."

"Whatever you say," he said, starting to get up.

She grabbed hold of his arm and pulled him back down and said, "I meant verbally."

He rolled over so that he was on top of her, and started using his tongue and mouth again. This time he worked his way down to the tangle of red hair between her legs, and brought her to a shattering climax with his tongue. By that time he was hard once more and drove himself into her again. She wrapped him in her arms and legs and held on tight until he went with her over the edge.

"Where will you start looking?" he asked as they lay snuggled together beneath the sheet.

"Colorado," she said. "That's where we heard he was when we were in Nevada. We spotted you soon after we

THE BOUNTY WOMEN 49

got to Utah, and hatched our little plot. It didn't do us much good, I'm afraid."

"It did *me* a lot of good," he said suggestively, and she nudged him with her elbow.

"At least we got to meet you," she said, basically agreeing with him. "I know that made the delay worth it for me. I can't speak for Sandy and Katy."

"You girls get along well, don't you?"

"Fairly well. Sandy's a little abrasive sometimes, and Katy's real quiet."

"And you?"

"I'm sort of in the middle."

"You're right up front, as far as I'm concerned," he told her.

"I'm glad," she said, nuzzling his neck. "I hope we see each other again, Clint."

"Well, you were sure the last time we parted company that we would. What about now?"

She placed her hand on his chest and said, "God, I hope so."

Anne left his room before morning, after they had made love several times more, but not before he made an effort to talk her out of going after Bill Wallmann.

"Whether or not Wallmann is the way you say, Anne, he's a very dangerous man. Do the three of you really think you can bring him in?"

"Sandy wants to bring him in dead, and Katy wants to bring him in alive. I just want to bring him in, but to answer your question, we hope that the three of us will be able to handle him."

"Now that you mention Sandy, I got the distinct impression earlier that she knew more about Wallmann than she was saying."

"You noticed that, huh? Yes, she knew Wallmann a couple of years ago—very well," she said, leaving no doubts about what she meant. "He walked away from her when she needed him, and she's never forgiven him."

"And she wants to kill him?"

"She's very bitter."

"She's got a lot of emotions churning inside of her, then, Anne. She ought to be too much of a pro for that, and you should be too much of a pro to ride with her in that condition."

"I know," was all Anne Archer would say, and Clint knew that she would go ahead and do it anyway.

"I can't talk you out of this?"

"I'm afraid not, Clint. If I backed away from every man who was dangerous, I wouldn't last very long in this business, would I?"

"No," he said, agreeing with her, but he refused to ask her how she had gotten into "this business" in the first place. It was like someone asking him why he had a reputation if he didn't like it.

"Then I won't try anymore," he said. "I'll just wish you luck."

"In a special way?" she asked, turning toward him.

"Yes," he said, taking her in his arms. "In a very special way."

After that, Anne left and Clint lay in bed alone, savoring the warmth she left behind, and feeling grateful for the opportunity to say good-bye without the others around. Actually, he wouldn't have minded saying good-bye to them as well, but if it had to be just one, he was glad it had been Anne. There was something truly special about her.

At first light he rose and walked to his window to watch the three of them ride out of town. Each woman in turn looked back at his hotel window, and he waved each time. Anne was the last to turn, and he waved to her, wondering if he'd ever see her—or any of them—again.

NINE

"Well, now that we've found him, how do we work this?" Anne Archer asked her two temporary partners.

They were all sitting astride their horses, looking down from a rise at a small cabin. The trail of Bill Wallmann had led them here, to the border between Colorado and Kansas. They had been sitting up there for hours and had finally caught sight of the man who was inhabiting the cabin. Sandy Spillane had positively identified him as Bill Wallmann.

"That's easy," Sandy said. "I'm going down there to talk to him. The two of you wait here."

"Now wait a minute—" Anne started to argue, but it was Katy Little Flower who cut her short.

"Anne, we agreed," Katy said. They had all agreed that Sandy—as the most experienced of the three, and because of her past association with Wallmann—would coordinate their manhunt.

"I know we did," Anne replied, "but to let her go down there alone—"

"He's not going to shoot me on sight," Sandy said with confidence.

"How do you know that?" Anne asked. "Everything we've learned about the man over the past couple of months indicates that he's changed drastically from the man you knew."

"That may be so, but although he left me, I never said that he didn't love me. He did. He just didn't want to be tied down." With unshaken confidence she said, "I know he'll talk to me."

"And then what?" Anne asked.

"Once I go inside with him, the two of you can come down and get the drop on him."

"It sounds too easy," Anne said.

"Don't be a pessimist," Sandy said. "Believe me, I'll have his undivided attention." Sandy raised her eyebrows at Anne and said, "Okay?"

"Yeah, sure," Anne said, still unconvinced but not the proud owner of a better idea.

"Katy?"

"I'm with you, Sandy."

"Good. Wish me luck."

Both girls did, and then Sandy started down toward the cabin.

"I don't like this," Anne said as they watched Sandy ride away.

"She knows what she's doing."

"Yeah."

As they watched, the door to the cabin opened when Sandy reached it, and Bill Wallmann—a tall, slim man dressed in black—stepped out. They exchanged words that Anne and Katy couldn't hear, and then Sandy got down off her horse and went inside with the gunman.

"That's it," Katy said.

"Give them a few minutes," Anne said quickly. "Let's make sure he's occupied."

After a few moments, both women became impatient. They dismounted and started down on foot to avoid any unplanned noises the horses might make.

"How are we going to do this part?" Katy asked.

"You take the back and I'll take the front. When we split up, we'll each count to twenty-five and then break in. Got it?"

"Right."

"Good luck," Anne said, and Katy nodded.

When they reached the front of the cabin, they split up and each began to count. Anne had reached twenty in her counting when she heard the first shot. Abandoning the plan, she opened the unlocked front door and leaped into the room.

Sandy Spillane was on the floor, gun in hand, and was trying to bring it to bear on Wallmann. The front of her shirt was covered with blood. The rear window shattered as Katy Little Flower burst through, and Wallmann quickly turned his attention that way and fired a shot. Anne heard Katy cry out as she pointed her own gun at Wallmann and fired—but he was no longer standing in the same spot. He had moved incredibly fast and avoided not only her bullet, but one fired at the same moment by Sandy Spillane as well. Sandy, with blood running down her arm, could not lift her gun for a second shot, and Katy Little Flower was sprawled facedown on the floor. That left it to Anne Archer.

Wallmann turned toward Anne with his gun in his hand, and stared at her.

"You want to take me?" he asked. Her heart was

pounding within her breast like something trying to get out, as he holstered his gun and said, "Go ahead, lady, take me."

TEN

The Gunsmith made his way through Utah by stopping at virtually every town he came to. He spent more time in some towns than in others, depending on the amount of business he was able to drum up.

A month after he parted company with the three women, he came to the border between Utah and Colorado and thought about them. As likely as not, they had entered Colorado a long time ago and had either caught Bill Wallmann or given up on catching him. Clint could have gone on east into Colorado now, or he could have gone north to Wyoming or south to New Mexico. He knew that he should have gone north or south, but he finally decided to go east, against his better judgment.

The first town Clint came to in Colorado was called Newton, and it was a fair-sized community. The prospects for some business were pretty good.

Clint put the rig and animals up at the livery, and went to the largest of the town's three hotels. While he was registering he just thought he'd ask the clerk if the three women had been in town during the past months.

"Oh sure," said the clerk, a man in his mid-twenties. "You couldn't miss three girls like that."

"No, you couldn't. How long ago were they here?"

The man shrugged and said, " 'Bout three weeks, give or take a day. You know them?"

"Our paths have crossed, yeah," Clint said. "I assume you've got bathing facilities?"

"Oh yes, sir, right in the back."

"Good. I'll drop my gear off in my room and be down for a bath."

"I'll have it prepared."

"Thanks. Make it hot."

Who am I kidding? he thought as he walked up to the second floor to find his room. He was curious about what had happened to the three female bounty hunters—especially Anne Archer—and that was why he'd asked about them. Since they had been in this town three weeks ago, it was obvious that he was traveling the same route they had, and sooner or later he'd come across some news concerning their hunt. He hoped he would find that they had finally abandoned their search for Wallmann, because if they found him, somebody was going to get hurt or—even more likely—killed. Wallmann would not be easy for a man to take, let alone three women.

After the bath, he followed his pattern over the past six weeks or so and found a saloon to settle down in for a while and relax before looking for some business.

He was starting on his second cold beer, seated at an out-of-the-way table, when a man walked into the saloon and approached the bar. He hadn't gotten a good look at the man's face, but from his profile he thought he looked familiar. He sipped his beer and watched the man's back at the bar while he ordered a drink, waiting for him to turn around.

The man finally turned with a beer in his hand, and spotted the Gunsmith at the same moment that Clint recognized him. He grinned and walked over to Clint's table.

"Jake Benteen," Clint said.

"Mind if I have a seat?"

"Be my guest."

Jake Benteen was not a big man by any stretch of the imagination, but Clint Adams knew he was a dangerous man. He was good with a gun—not fast, but he generally hit what he aimed at—and he *was* fast with his fists. Clint had seen him in action on more than one occasion.

He was also a bounty hunter.

"You working?" Clint asked.

"Almost always."

"Not last year, when Lacy was in Wyoming, hunting bear."

"As it turned out," Benteen said, "I was—but that's a long story. I was in the wrong place at the right time—or vice versa."

"Works that way sometimes."

"Lacy told me about the hunt," Benteen said.

Clint didn't bother asking if she had told him everything. Lacy Blake was Benteen's partner, only last year she'd been working solo when she and Clint Adams had been hunting "Ole Three-Paw," a monstrous grizzly who was tearing up the stock of ranchers in Bear Pass, Wyoming.*

"Lacy meeting you?" Clint asked.

Benteen shook his head and said, "She's gone off somewhere. She does that sometimes."

The Gunsmith #24: Killer Grizzly

"So do you, I've heard."

Benteen shrugged and said, "We have a flexible relationship."

"So I understand. Tell me, what—or who—brings you to this part of Colorado?"

"Passing through."

"On your way to where?"

Benteen answered with a tight grin over the rim of his beer mug. He was the close-mouthed type, always figuring that if he revealed whom he was hunting, someone else might get there first and beat him to the bounty.

"Let me guess, then," Clint said.

"Take your best shot."

"Bill Wallmann."

The look on Benteen's face as he put his mug down told Clint he'd hit it right on the head the first time.

"Is the price on him really five thousand?"

"It is. I heard you were out of the business," Benteen said. "Still keeping up on posters?"

"No. I've got some friends who mentioned it to me."

"Pros?"

"Not in your league, but yeah, they're pros."

Benteen made a face and said, "They talk too much. Who are we talking about?"

"Anne Archer, Sandy Spillane and Katy Little Flower."

"Spillane I know," Benteen said, frowning. "She was with Wallmann for a while until he dumped her. She out for the price on his head or revenge?"

"Both, I guess.

"I don't know the other two."

"They seemed—competent."

"I've only known one woman who made a good bounty hunter, and that's because I taught her."

Benteen was talking about his partner, Lacy Blake.

"On the whole, they're too emotional, and Spillane is carrying around more than most. I don't know her two friends, but they ought to get shed of her quick."

"I guess you're right. You staying in town?"

Benteen shook his head and said, "Just stopped to wash away some old dust to make room for the new." With that he lifted his mug and drained it, and pushed back his chair to leave. He stopped short, though, and Clint could see that he had something on his mind.

"You sure you're out of it?"

"I'm just traveling around mending guns, Jake."

Benteen nodded to himself, still wrestling with a decision.

"I heard some news from the other end of the state," he said finally.

"Something I'd be interested in?"

"Probably. I heard three bounty hunters tried to take Wallmann and he shot 'em up."

"Killed them?" Clint asked, with a cold feeling in the pit of his stomach.

"Didn't hear that," Benteen said, rising, "but I figured I'd best tell you what I did hear."

Clint nodded and said, "Thanks, Jake."

"I guess I'll be seeing you," Benteen said, "sooner or later."

"Yeah," Clint said, staring down at the tabletop.

"I'll say hello to Lacy for you, when I see her."

Clint looked at Benteen and said, "I appreciate that, Jake."

He watched Benteen leave and wondered idly what the outcome would be when he caught up with Wallmann. He put that thought aside, however, and thought more about what Benteen had told him. Of course, it could have been any three bounty hunters that Wallmann had "shot up," but they didn't usually travel in packs.

It had to be the three women, and for all he knew, they were all dead.

There was only one way to find out.

ELEVEN

All Benteen had told him was that the incident had taken place at the other end of the state. That could have meant a lot of things. It could have been on the border between Colorado and Kansas, or farther north, on the Nebraska border. The only thing he could hope for was that on the way he'd come up with more information that would help him pinpoint it.

The decision to leave his rig and team in Newton was a difficult one. He didn't know the town or anyone in it, and he had to rely on the honesty of the liveryman. Of course, he paid the man well enough to care for his possessions while he was gone, and promised to match the amount when he returned. He also told the man that if he didn't return, everything was to be sent to Labyrinth, Texas, and he would be paid well for taking care of that. He had to leave the rig behind, though, because he just wouldn't be able to make any time with it. With Duke, on the other hand, he could travel faster than anyone. For speed and stamina, he'd put Duke up against the best horse in the country.

As he left Newton, he told himself it wasn't Bill Wallmann he was looking for, it was the three women. He wanted to find out if they were the three bounty hunters he'd heard about, and if so, how badly they had been "shot up." In the back of his mind he knew it was Anne Archer he was most concerned about.

However, he still had no intention of hunting down Bill Wallmann for bounty, no matter what had happened to Anne or the others.

That was what he kept telling himself.

TWELVE

Clint decided to travel in a straight line that, if he found no information to cause him to deviate from it, would take him to the Kansas border.

He stopped in every town, but only long enough to check on whether or not the three women had passed through during their manhunt. As long as the answer was consistently yes, he knew he was still heading in the right direction.

He slept under the stars in order to get an early start each morning, and he covered so much ground that he was somewhat surprised he hadn't caught up with Jake Benteen, who had not quite a day's head start on him.

Truth to tell, however, he was also glad he had *not* crossed paths with Benteen. He wasn't sure that the bounty hunter—possibly the best in the business—would believe that he was not after the price on Bill Wallmann's head.

Finally Clint came across definite information as to the three women's whereabouts. A lawman in a town called

Willow Crossing gave it to him after finding out that he was the Gunsmith.

"Sure, Mr. Adams," the awed lawman said. "I heard that Wallmann tangled with three women over to Dry Creek. That's just off the Kansas border."

"What kind of shape were they left in?"

"All I know for sure is that one of them was killed and the other two was shot up."

"You know which one was killed?"

"Couldn't tell you that 'cause I don't know any of their names, just that they was hunting bounty. Shoot, that's a man's job, don't they know that? Well," the sheriff said, answering his own question, "I guess they do now, huh?"

"I guess so," Clint said, looking at the elderly, overweight lawman with distaste.

"You going after Wallmann? Wouldn't that be some showdown, the Gunsmith and Bill Wallmann."

"Sorry to disappoint you, Sheriff," Clint said, "but I'm just concerned with the condition of my friends."

"Them girls friends of yours?"

"Yes."

"And you're gonna let Wallmann get away with shooting them up that way?" The lawman looked puzzled. "That don't go with your rep."

"A reputation is just so much bullshit, Sheriff," Clint said with annoyance. "You're a lawman—I'm surprised you don't know that."

The Gunsmith turned on his heel and left the lawman's office, and the old sheriff said aloud, "Shit, I ain't never had no rep to find out from. Shee-it!"

Clint hurried to the town of Dry Creek, Colorado—a three-hour ride from Willow Crossing—and immediately sought out the town doctor, who turned out to be a crusty old codger named Dewey, who had to be at least eighty.

"Sure I remember treating them fillies," he told Clint. "I may be an old cuss, but I still appreciate good-looking females, and them three was sure good-looking."

"They *were* good-looking? I heard that one of them was killed."

"You heard wrong, son," the old man said.

"You mean more than one? Or all? Was the one of them named—"

"Give me a chance to explain and I'll tell ya!"

"All right," Clint said. "Explain."

"Wasn't none of them killed, sonny. Oh, one of them was knocking real hard on them pearly gates, but she's lucky she had me tending her and not one of these young whippersnappers with their newfangled ways of doing things."

"Well then, how are they? Where are they?"

"They're over to the hotel, in separate rooms."

Clint rushed out of the doctor's office without even asking which one had been seriously injured.

When he got to the hotel—the only one in the small border town—he asked the clerk what rooms the three women were in.

"We don't answer questions like that hereabouts, mister. People got a right to their—ohh!!"

Clint had grabbed the man by the collar and twisted until his face was turning blue, then loosened his grip enough to let him talk.

"You want to talk to me now?"

"Top of the stairs, three rooms on the right side. We only got six in the whole place."

Clint let the man go and said, "Thanks."

He went upstairs, and when he reached the first room he tried the knob and found the door unlocked. If he had knocked, the person in the bed would not have been able to let him in, anyway.

He approached the bed and breathed a sigh of relief when he saw that it was not Anne Archer, but Katy Little Flower—and then felt guilty for the thought.

"Clint!" a voice said from behind him, and he turned to find Anne standing in the door.

"Hello, Anne."

She looked harried, but still lovely. She was carrying a basin of water and had a couple of towels draped over her arm, so she walked to the dresser and put them down, then turned to him and moved into the circle of his arms. He could feel her body quivering, and he knew it was not from lust.

"I haven't given in to it yet," she said, with her face buried in his chest.

"It's all right," he said. "You're okay."

"Yes, I am," she said. "Now. I think I knew all along that you'd come."

"I'm here."

They stood like that for a few moments, and then he said, "Do you want to tell me what happened?"

She pushed away from him and said, "While I take care of Katy."

"Where's Sandy?"

"In the next room," she said, wetting a towel from the basin so she could mop Katy's brow. "She was hit in the shoulder, but Katy almost died."

"Tell me about it."

Anne explained how they had tracked Wallmann to the cabin, and then how Sandy had gone down first.

"Alone?"

"She thought she could handle him."

"And she was wrong."

"Yes. He wouldn't believe that she had come looking for him because she loved him. She kept trying to convince him, and then he told her to leave, and Sandy went for her gun."

She went on to explain how she had gone through the cabin's front door, and Katy had broken through the rear window.

"That's how she got the cuts on her face," she said, and Clint, taking his first good look at the woman in the bed, saw that her face was cut in several places.

"Wallmann fired from reflex, I think, catching her in the belly, and then he moved. God, I've never seen anyone move that fast. Sandy and I fired, and I swear he dodged the bullets. Sandy passed out then, and it was just Wallmann and me." She shivered at the memory.

"What happened?"

"He asked me if I wanted to take him, then holstered his gun and said to go ahead."

"He wanted you to draw on him?"

"Yes, and I couldn't." She was sitting on the bed next to her friend, and looked up at him. "Clint, I froze. I swear to God, I've never been that scared in my life. And do you know what he did?"

"Yes," Clint said. "He left."

"That's exactly what he did. He just walked past me out the door, and while I was trying to take care of Sandy and Katy, I heard him ride away." She started wiping Katy's face again and said, "I still don't know how I got back here with the two of them."

"Determination."

He saw the slump in her shoulders and said, "You think you showed cowardice?"

She put her hands in her lap and asked, "What would you call it?"

"Good sense, honey," he said, putting his hand on her shoulder. "Damned good sense."

THIRTEEN

While Anne continued to care for Katy, Clint went to the next room to see Sandy. Anne assured him that she was awake and able to talk.

"If she wants to," Anne added. "She's been very quiet since we got back, and you know that's not like her at all."

"Yes, I know. Let's see if she'll talk to me."

"I'll be by soon."

"What's Katy's condition, Anne?"

"The belly wound took a lot out of her, Clint. She's awake sometimes, but sometimes she doesn't know where she is. The doc says she'll start improving, but I keep wondering when."

"And Sandy?"

"Her shoulder was pretty bad. It's only been two and a half weeks, maybe three. It'll still be a while before she can ride."

"And what are you going to do?"

She looked at him then and said, "I'm going after him."

"That's what I thought."

She shrugged, smiled at him and said, "Can't show good sense all the time, can we?"

"I guess not," he said. "I'll go talk to Sandy."

He left the room and walked to the next one, where Sandy was sitting up in bed.

"Clint Adams," she said when she saw him in the doorway.

"Hello, Sandy."

"Come to say 'I told you so'?" she asked bitterly.

"Came to see how you are."

"Piss-poor," she said.

"Want to talk?"

Sandy compressed her full lips and stared off into space.

"You've got to talk to somebody, Sandy."

She continued to stare and then suddenly said, "Close the door, will you?"

He shut it and then approached the bed.

"Sit here," she said, patting the bed with her good hand. "If we're gonna talk, you might as well sit.

"I hate to admit this—and I'll deny it if you tell anyone—but when I got in that shack with Bill I felt like a schoolgirl. I forgot everything I've taught myself over the past five years, and it almost got us all killed."

"Don't punish yourself, Sandy," Clint said. "It's obvious you loved the man once. That's not an easy thing to forget."

"Yes, I loved him, and I thought I hated him now—until I saw him. When he told me to leave, it was like it was happening all over again."

THE BOUNTY WOMEN

"And you went for your gun."

She laughed ironically and said, "I messed up and went for my gun instead of waiting for Anne and Katy, and look what happened."

Clint recalled what Jake Benteen had said about women having too much emotion to make good bounty hunters. He had been more right than he knew.

"He put a hole in me before I could even touch my gun," she said, shaking her head. "He's even faster than I remembered."

"He's fast, all right," Clint said. "Maybe the fastest."

"Faster than you?"

Clint shrugged and stood up.

"You'd better get all the rest you can."

"I don't have time for that," she said. "Anne's going after him, and I can't let her go alone."

"You rest up," Clint said. "She won't be going alone."

"You mean—?"

"I mean just what I said," he said, heading for the door. "Now get some rest."

"Do you mean it?" Anne asked.

"Yes."

"But why did you change your mind?"

"You."

"What did I say?"

"You said you were going after him alone," Clint said. "I couldn't let you do that, so my options were clear. Either talk you out of it, or go with you. I can't talk you out of it, can I?"

"No."

"Then I'll go with you."

"Oh, Clint," she said, putting both hands on his arm. Katy Little Flower was oblivious to what was going on. "I don't know how to thank you."

"Before you try, let me tell you my conditions."

"Conditions?"

"Yes."

Frowning, Anne asked, "What conditions?"

"We're bringing him back alive."

"Alive?" Anne said, looking at Katy lying in bed, hovering somewhere between life and death.

"Revenge is what did that to Katy," Clint said, "and to Sandy. We're not out for revenge, we're just out to bring in a wanted man."

"Alive."

"Yes."

"If possible."

Clint stared at her and said, "I intend to do my damnedest to make it possible."

"Is that the only condition?"

"One more. We'll do this my way, Anne."

She grinned at him and said, "Haven't we always done things your way?"

Remembering her inventiveness in bed, he smiled back and said, "Not hardly."

FOURTEEN

The first thing they did after the agreement was made was to check out the horses in the livery.

"Which of the three of you has the best horse?" he asked, although he'd already formulated his own opinion.

"Much as I like my dun," she said, "Katy's paint is the best. He's the fastest and fittest."

"That's what I thought. I notice she doesn't ride with a saddle."

"No."

"Will he take one?"

"I think so."

"Can you ride him?"

"Yes."

"Then you'll take him, and we'll arrange for a packhorse."

"Why a packhorse? We can stop in towns along the—"

"If we stop in a town, word could get around. Wallmann will learn that we're on his trail. More than that, somebody might recognize me, and then he'll know who's on his trail. If we stay away from towns, we'll have an advantage over him."

"You think he knew that we were coming?" Anne asked, referring to herself and her two partners.

"Individually the three of you are not exactly unnoticeable; together you're downright impossible to miss. Yeah, I'm sure he knew."

"Then when Sandy rode up to that cabin, he knew she wasn't alone."

"That's what I figure."

She shook her head and said, "And we thought we were pros."

"You will be."

"How naïve we were."

"You'll learn," he said, and mentally added, *You'll learn or end up dead.* "Just for the record, Anne," he went on, "I don't think this is any business for a woman."

"But you—"

"I'm just telling you what I think. I'm entitled to that, aren't I?"

"Yes."

"You've been at it for three years, Sandy for five. That isn't long enough to know anything, Anne. I was a lawman for eighteen years, and there's still plenty I *never* learned. That's the first thing *you've* got to learn—you'll never know all there is to know."

Sheepishly she said, "All right."

"Acquaint yourself with that paint," he said. "I'll arrange for a packhorse and buy the supplies. We'll be leaving at first light."

He started out of the livery, then turned and said, "I'll see you back at the hotel. I'll buy you dinner."

THE BOUNTY WOMEN

"Whatever you say, Clint," she said. "You're the boss."

After dinner they went to her room in the hotel. Ostensibly she had moved in with Katy because there weren't any rooms left, and she told the clerk to give Clint hers. Technically, then, they were in his room and in his bed.

"I'm glad you decided to go with me," she said with her head on his chest. They had just made love and were both covered with a fine sheen of sweat.

"I'm doing it to keep you alive," he said, tightening his arms around her.

"That's the only reason?"

"That's it."

She wondered if that meant he loved her, but she knew better than to ask. As she kissed him eagerly, she knew that she would be content with whatever he gave her.

In the morning Clint awoke first and went out to load the supplies onto the packhorse. When Anne awoke, she checked on Katy and Sandy, and found Sandy on her feet.

"What do you think you're doing?" she demanded angrily.

"Simmer down, Annie," Sandy said. "While you're off with Clint having a good time, somebody's got to see to Katy."

"Having a good—"

"I didn't mean that," Sandy said quickly. "I know what you're doing, Anne, and why. Be careful." She approached Anne and touched her shoulder. "Don't go off half-cocked like I did."

"Clint won't let me do that," she said.

"No," Sandy replied, "I don't suppose he will. I only

hope he's as good with a gun as they say he is, because I *know* Bill Wallmann is."

"I'll be there to help him," Anne said.

"Honey, if it comes right down to those two, you better just butt out and let them have at it. Men like those two, they wouldn't have it any other way."

"Clint's not like that."

"Don't fool yourself, my girl. They're all like that," Sandy said, "even if they don't know it."

FIFTEEN

The first night they camped in Kansas, Clint told Anne about Jake Benteen.

"I've heard of him," she said. "He rides with a woman partner, doesn't he?"

"Sometimes," he said. "Lacy Blake."

She looked sharply at him, but although she thought she detected something in his voice when he said Lacy Blake's name, his face betrayed nothing.

"She's supposed to be good."

"She learned from the best."

"Benteen?"

"You must know he's probably the best bounty hunter around," he said.

"I suppose."

"He may do this for us."

"I hope not."

"Revenge again?"

She shook her head and said, "Five thousand dollars. Speaking of which—"

"I don't want any," he said, knowing what she was going to say. "You can split it evenly with Sandy and Katy."

"But—"

"But you can't split anything if we don't catch him."

"How are we supposed to know where he went?"

"We don't. We'll stop in some towns and see if we can pick up any information."

"I thought we weren't going to stay in any towns?"

"We're not. We'll alternate going to a town and hanging around, keeping our ears open. A few hours ought to do it."

"Do we ask anybody?"

"No. That's the best way to bring attention to yourself. Lord knows, you're noticeable enough as it is."

"I'll take that as a compliment."

"When you go to town," Clint said, "all you're to do is listen. Understand?"

"I understand."

Clint went into a town first, leaving Anne with the packhorse and supplies. The town was called Blue Ridge, and all he did while he was there was sit in the saloons, biding his time in each over a single beer, and listening to talk.

He did this in Blue Ridge, Clifford and Rawlings.

Anne did it in the towns of Sentinel, Bradley and Split Fork.

Finally, while Clint was in Bolten, he heard a townsman mention that Wallmann had been seen in Wichita.

"Man's gotta have balls to show up in a big town like that with a price on his head," the man said.

Clint listened closely, but there was no further mention of Wallmann, and he left town and reached the camp as darkness was falling. Anne already had a fire going and dinner cooking.

"Welcome home," she said as he dismounted.

"Got some word," he said. "I'll tell you about it after I tend to Duke."

"Dinner should be ready by then."

It was by unspoken agreement that Anne would do the cooking after the first night they camped. She had told Clint that she didn't like brittle, burnt bacon and strong coffee.

"I'll give up the brittle bacon, but not the coffee," he said.

After that the bacon was not so well done, but the coffee remained strong.

When he returned to the fire she handed him a plate of bacon and beans and asked, "What did you learn?"

"Wallmann was seen in Wichita."

"That doesn't make sense. Wichita is not a small town. How would he have the nerve to go there with five thousand dollars on his head?"

Clint shrugged and said, "What would you think if you saw him walking down the street in Wichita?"

She thought a moment, then said, "I'd probably think I saw someone who looked like Bill Wallmann."

"Right. Who'd expect him to go to Wichita? Which is probably just why he did go."

"If it was him."

"Well, the only way we're going to find out is to go there and check it out."

"After we eat?"

He nodded and said, "In the morning."

SIXTEEN

Outside Wichita, Clint said, "We won't ride in together. You go in first, and I'll follow. You cover the south end of town and I'll cover the north. Same routine, keep your ears open and listen. If he was here, we have to figure out if he went toward Missouri or Oklahoma."

"Maybe we should split up."

"First let's see what we find out, Anne, and then we'll decide."

Actually he had already decided, and as he watched her ride ahead of him to enter Wichita first, he knew that he had no intention of splitting up. His whole aim in coming was to keep her from facing Wallmann alone, and that was what he intended to do.

When Clint rode into Wichita, he did not even bother to look for Anne Archer. They were to meet outside of town just before dark to compare notes.

He found a livery on his side of town, put Duke up and

then began hitting the saloons. It wasn't long before he heard what he was hoping to hear.

"Yeah," a man was saying as he entered one of the saloons, "it's the talk of the town, all right. Imagine Bill Wallmann daring to come here with a price that high on his head."

"What's the price now?" another man asked.

"Five thousand, but I heard that they're talking 'bout raising it to six since he shot up three bounty hunters a few weeks back."

"Three bounty hunters?"

"Yeah, but I heard they was women."

"*Women* bounty hunters, trying to take Bill Wallmann? That's crazy."

The voices were blending together, but who was talking didn't matter so much as what they were saying. Clint ordered a beer and stood at the bar to drink it so he could continue to listen.

"Nobody can take Wallmann, especially not with a gun," someone said. "The only man who could've stood up to Wallmann with a gun was ol' Bill Hickok."

"What about the Gunsmith? Wasn't he supposed to be as fast as Hickok?"

"Ah, I heard he quit, put his gun away."

"Reckon he lost his nerve?"

"Possible, I guess. Rep like that gets mighty heavy after a while."

The speaker didn't know the half of it.

"Anyway, where was Wallmann headed when he was last seen?"

"Somebody said they heard somebody say that he was headed for Oklahoma."

"Sounds like a lot of somebodies," somebody said.

They all laughed and the conversation turned itself to

another course. Clint finished his beer and left the saloon.

"Somebody said" was really all he could hope to go on, unless . . . unless he changed his own plan and went and talked to the law in town. He quickly decided against that. He and Anne could ride into Oklahoma, and the first town they hit should be able to tell them the story. If Wallmann had passed through, Clint was sure they'd still be talking about it.

Clint decided to pass the time until he had to meet Anne by simply walking the streets of the town. As he walked, he wondered idly how close Benteen was to Wallmann's trail. Surely the bounty hunter had to be between them and the wanted man. Would he get there first? Clint couldn't work up any regrets if the man did. Wallmann would be in custody and Anne would be alive, even if she didn't have a third of five thousand dollars.

That might not satisfy her, but it sure would satisfy him.

SEVENTEEN

Anne heard pretty much the same thing Clint did in one of the saloons she visited, but as she was leaving a man suddenly took a liking to the way she looked.

"Hey, little miss," he said, grabbing her left arm as she walked past his table. "Set a while and visit, why don't you?"

"Let go of me."

"Come on, pretty lady," the man said. He was a big man, but he was carrying a lot of years of beer around his waist. "Don't be in such a hurry."

"Mister, I said let go. Now you either do it yourself or I'll have to make you."

"Whoa!" the man said, looking at his two friends who were seated with him at the table. "This little lady talks big, don't she?"

"The little lady backs up what she says," Anne said, and the would-be Romeo didn't realize that she had her gun out until she cocked it. At the sound he turned his head quickly and almost impaled his nose on the barrel of her gun.

"Now either you turn loose my arm or I'm gonna give you a third nostril, friend."

The coldness of her tone and of her eyes cooled the man's ardor and he loosened his grip on her arm, looking embarrassed.

"That's fine," she said, taking a step or two to remove herself from his reach. "Much obliged."

She holstered her gun and strode out of the saloon.

"Will," the man said to one of the other men at the table, "see where that little lady goes. She's got something to answer for, and I think after dark will be a good time for her to do it."

The man called Will nodded, rose and left the saloon in Anne Archer's wake.

Anne was so intent on meeting Clint and telling him what she'd heard that she didn't notice the man on her tail.

Clint reached the meeting place first and watched as Anne rode towards him. Behind her he could see some dust, and the figure of a man on a horse. Anne had picked up some company, and she looked to be totally unaware of it.

"I've got some information," she said excitedly as she reached him.

"So do I," he said, still looking behind her. "You've got a friend."

"What?" she said. She saw the direction in which he was looking, and turned to take a look herself. They both watched as the man wheeled his horse around and rode back to town.

"Who was that?" she asked.

"I don't know, but he was following you, that's for sure. Anything happen in town?"

"Not much," she said, and then told him about the incident in the saloon.

"I guess that's it, then," Clint said. "You embarrassed the man in front of his friends. Some men don't forget that."

"So why follow me and then turn back? Because he saw you?"

"My guess is he just wanted to know what direction you were heading in."

"South," she said, "to Oklahoma."

Clint looked at her and said, "That's what I heard, too."

"Then let's go."

"It's close to dark," he said, looking up at the sky. "We'll ride a ways and then make camp. I think we'll have to be on the lookout for your friends, though."

"You think they'll come after us?"

"I think if one of them went so far as to follow you, we can expect a visit."

"That's all we need," she said glumly. "As if we didn't have enough problems."

"It's your fault."

"What? I didn't invite him—"

"You're just too damn good-looking for your own good, Anne," he said. "Next time I let you go into town, we're going to have to do something about that."

"Like what?"

"I don't know," he answered. "Let's get a move on, and I'll think about it."

EIGHTEEN

When they were camped and having dinner around the fire, they were about a day's ride from Oklahoma, a state that held some fond memories for the Gunsmith—and some that were not so fond.

"I wore a badge for the first time in Oklahoma," he told Anne, "and I asked a girl to marry me for the first time."

"Did she?"

"No."

"What happened?"

"Problems arose," he said.* "It's too long a story to tell now."

After dinner, Anne noticed that Clint's head was cocked, as if he were listening to something.

"What is it?"

"I thought I heard something."

"Like what?"

---

*The Gunsmith #2: The Chinese Gunmen, and The Gunsmith #3: The Woman Hunt

He hesitated a moment, still listening, then said, "I'm not sure. Maybe a horse—maybe nothing."

She cocked her head now, in an effort to hear what he heard, and asked, "Do you think it's those men from town?"

"I don't know," he answered, "but just to be on the safe side, I'd better stand watch."

"We'll split the watch, of course," she said.

"Of course. I'll wake you when I get tired."

"Maybe I'll sit with you a while."

"All that would do is distract me. Go to sleep."

"All right, but you'd better wake me."

"I will, I will. Good night."

She nodded, went over to her bedroll and curled up with her rifle. Clint waited just long enough for her to fall asleep, and then made his move.

He knew that he had not only heard horses but that he'd smelled bacon as well—and Anne had not cooked any bacon. His plan was to wait until Anne was asleep, and then backtrack on foot and see who was on their trail.

He didn't bother taking his rifle along because he figured he could handle whatever came along with his modified Colt.

Clint followed with his nose and ears the smell of bacon and coffee, along with the occasional sound made by the horses. Eventually he knew he was getting closer because he was able to discern voices, although he couldn't understand what they were saying yet.

Suddenly he was able to make out the glow of a campfire, and the voices were now clearer. He moved in a bit closer, until he was able not only to understand what was being said, but to see who was speaking.

There were three men sitting around the fire, drinking coffee now and talking. He couldn't tell if any of them had

THE BOUNTY WOMEN 93

been the rider following Anne, but after listening to their conversation for a few moments, he decided that it had been one of them.

"When will we move in on them?" one man asked another, larger man who was apparently the leader.

"I don't rightly know," the larger man answered. "Guess I ain't made up my mind yet. All I know is she's gonna pay for making a fool outta me when all I wanted was to be a little friendly."

Clint decided to step in and nip the man's plans in the bud.

"I can understand why she didn't want to be friendly," he said, stepping from the darkness into the glow of the fire. "I can smell you all the way over here."

"Wha—?" the big man said, gaping at him. "Who the hell are you?"

The other two men started to get up, but Clint said, "Just sit tight, gentlemen, and nobody will get hurt."

Something in his voice made them sit back down on the ground.

"Whaddaya want?" the larger man asked.

"Your name."

"My name?"

"Yeah, yours," Clint said. "The fat one."

"Mister, you're looking for trouble."

"No, you're the one looking for trouble. You've been following me and my fiancé."

"Fancy—what?"

"Fee-on-say," Clint said again, saying it slowly. "The girl I'm going to marry."

"Marry?"

"Are you the oaf who grabbed her in Wichita?" Clint asked, making his tone even harder. "Because if you are, I'm going to put some holes in you, friend."

"I didn't grab nobody—" the man started to protest, but then he suddenly realized that there were three of them and only one stranger.

"Listen, boys," he said aloud, "there's three of us and one of him. We can take him."

Before the other men could answer, Clint said, "Not even on the best day of your lives, boys. Don't try it."

The two men exchanged glances, looking totally confused. Whoever this fellow was, he wasn't afraid to face down three men, and that made him either crazy or damned fast with that gun!

"Don't let him bluff you."

"I'm not bluffing anybody, mister," Clint said. "I'm not even concerned with these fellas. My concern is you. If you don't mount up and head back the way you came, you're in for some serious trouble that you aren't ever going to recover from."

"Who the hell are you?"

"Now if I was to tell you that, it would take all the fun out of this."

"I wanna know."

Clint shrugged and said, "My name's Clint Adams."

"Jesus," one of the other men said in a hushed voice. "The Gunsmith."

"See?" Clint said, looking directly at the big man. "It's all ruined."

"Hey, mister," one of the other men said, "we didn't mean nothing, we was just doing what Dirk said—"

"Dirk," Clint repeated. "Is that you, fat man? Is that your name?"

"That's him," the third man said. "Dirk White."

"Okay, Dirk White, here's the way it plays," Clint said. "I knew you were here because I smelled you. If I smell you again, you're dead." He looked at the other two men in turn and said, "That goes for you too. If I smell *him*, you're both dead."

"Hey, that ain't fair!" one of them yelled.

Clint shrugged and said, "Too bad. That's the way it is."

"Don't worry, Mr. Adams," the third man said, "you ain't gonna smell him."

"Good," Clint said, "because I've had about all I can stand anyway."

Dirk White didn't move at all until Clint Adams melted into the darkness, and then he looked at his two companions.

"There's still three of us and one of him."

"Oh no, Dirk," one man said. "There's one of you and one of him, and if you feel lucky, be our guest."

Both men got up and went to saddle their horses. Dirk White considered calling them cowards, but decided instead to get up and saddle his horse too.

As Clint reached his own campfire, he heard the click of a hammer being cocked and called out, "Whoa, it's me."

When Anne saw him she uncocked her gun and holstered it, staring at him.

"Where were you?"

"Visiting friends."

"What friends?"

"Your friends," he said. "The one who grabbed you, the one who followed you, and a third man."

"You faced the three of them?"

"It wasn't hard," he said, smiling. "I talked tough."

"You *talked?* You didn't draw your gun?"

"I only draw my gun when I'm going to use it," he told her.

"So what happened?"

"Nothing. They're on their way back to Wichita, and we're on our way to Oklahoma. Let's get some sleep."
"No more watch?"
"No," he lied, "no more watch."
He lay awake, all senses alert, while she slept.

NINETEEN

When they crossed into Oklahoma, Anne asked Clint a question that had been on her mind for a while.

"How long will you stay with this?"

"The hunt?"

She nodded.

It was not a question that he hadn't asked himself a few times, most recently the night before while lying awake. If Wallmann kept going into Texas and on through to Mexico, they could be on his trail for weeks, maybe months.

Unless . . .

"I've got an idea."

"That doesn't answer my question," Anne said.

"I guess I can take it as long as you can," he said, "but maybe we won't have to."

"What's your idea?"

"When we get to the next town, I'm going to send some telegrams. I've got some friends in Texas—"

"Not Oklahoma?"

"Oklahoma's part of my past," he said. "Texas is part of my present, and I've got some friends there."

"So?"

"So I'll send some telegrams asking my friends to keep an eye out for Wallmann. Eventually we may get some idea which way he's heading, and we might be able to get ahead of him."

"Ahead of him? You mean, take a shortcut and end up waiting for him to come to us?"

"Sure, why not?"

"Do you know any shortcuts?"

"There are always shortcuts," he said. "Once we've got him spotted, we'll find one—or we'll make one."

Happily for Clint, their path did not take them through the town of Stratton, Oklahoma. Too many memories there. Instead, they rode into the town of Flatrock which, although it was not large, did have a telegraph office.

"What about riding in together?" Anne asked as they dismounted in front of the telgraph office.

"We won't be here long enough for word to get out. Just to be safe, though, don't come inside with me. Wait here."

"I can wait in the saloon."

"No, I don't want you making any more new friends like Dirk White."

"That wasn't my fault!"

"I know. Wait for me here."

"I need something cold to drink."

"Wait for me here," he said again, "and we'll go to a cafe and have some lemonade."

"Lemonade? I want a beer."

"I don't want you anywhere near a saloon. Now will you please just wait here?"

"Yes sir."

"Thank you."

Clint went inside, drafted a telegram and sent basically the same message to the towns of Labyrinth and Lansdale, Texas. He knew that his friends in those towns would in turn send their own telegrams in an effort to pinpoint Bill Wallmann's direction of travel.

When he reappeared outside he was relieved to find Anne waiting for him.

"Let's go get that lemonade."

"Ugh!"

In the cafe they sat at a table and each had a tall glass of lemonade.

"I've got to ask," he said finally.

"What?"

"How you got in this business."

"You ask that of your whores, too?"

"I don't use whores," he said, very seriously.

"I'm sorry. That was a silly thing to say. Are you really interested in why I'm a bounty hunter?"

"Yes."

"All right." She took a few moments to formulate her thoughts. "I did it, I think, because I didn't want to end up drinking this stuff all the time," she said, holding up her glass of lemonade.

"What?"

"I grew up in a mid-sized town, Clint, and it was growing when I left. It had a church, and a woman's civic group—I didn't want to end up marrying some poor fool and living in that town my whole life, baking pies for the church and drinking lemonade with the ladies of the town. Do you know what I mean?"

"I think so."

"I'm twenty-five. I left that town when I was eighteen,

and for four years I traveled. I worked in banks, general stores, saloons—I was never a whore," she added quickly.

"I didn't think you were."

"But I did work in saloons. It was while I was working in one that I met Sandy. She was looking for a man with a price on his head, and I had seen him in the saloon. She wanted me to tell her where he was, but I said I'd take her to him. She shared the money with me, and I've been a bounty hunter ever since."

"Is it a better life than you would have had in your hometown?"

"Yes," she said without even hesitating.

"You could have been killed in that cabin with Sandy and Katy."

"It's still worth it. I'm drinking this because I want to," she said, indicating the half-empty glass of lemonade, "not because I have to, not because I have to be one of the ladies."

With that she put the glass down and pushed it away.

"Ugh!"

TWENTY

Bill Wallmann was a confused man—and although he would never admit it, he was very probably a frightened man as well.

For years Bill Wallmann had killed for money. He was nearly forty years old, and he had been killing men for money for more than half his life. He had never, however, been a bounty hunter. He was paid to *kill*, pure and simple, with no pretense of seeking any kind of justice. Very rarely did he kill for any other reason, and when he did it was in self-defense.

Clint Adams had said that Bill Wallmann was not an indiscriminate killer, and he was right. He was hired, pointed at someone—much the way a gun is pointed—and then paid.

Of late, however, Wallmann had changed, and even he was at something of a loss to explain it. His temper had quickened, and with it his trigger finger, and he could no longer control either one.

Wallmann was on his way to Mexico, where he was

going to hide out and try to figure out what was happening to him. Usually his bouts of quick temper had been accompanied by brutal headaches, so perhaps the problem was medical, but if there was anything in the world that Bill Wallmann feared—and he'd never admit that there was—it was doctors. The only time he had ever let a doctor near him was to remove a bullet, and then only with the greatest reluctance and because he'd had no choice.

The incident that had decided Wallmann to go to Mexico was what he had done to Sandy Spillane in that cabin. Before he could stop himself, he was shooting, and then he had challenged the other girl to draw on him! Luckily she had not, and he had come to his senses and left her standing there.

Wallmann was on his way to Mexico, and if anyone got in his way, he knew what was going to happen—and he would be helpless to stop it!

TWENTY-ONE

"Anything?" Anne asked.

Clint had just returned from another town where he had checked in with the telegraph operator for messages.

"No, nothing . . . yet," he said, adding the last word after a moment. He didn't want Anne to become discouraged—and yet if she did, maybe she'd give it up. If she was willing to give up the hunt, he certainly was—but he doubted that would ever happen. The way she felt, that would be letting down Sandy, Katy and herself.

"What if he's not ahead of us?" she said. "What if he went east, or west?"

"Let's sit and talk about it. I've got some ideas to throw your way."

"Fine."

When they were settled around a fire with coffee, he began to talk.

"Let's say I'm a gunman—and I know my reputation says I am—"

"I didn't say anything," she protested.

"I know. I wanted to say it first—but let's say I'm a gunman with a price on my head, with bounty hunters on my trail. Where am I going to go?"

"Mexico," she said immediately, and surprised even herself.

"Why did you say that?"

"Because it was the first place that came to my mind."

"Right. Get out of the country until things cool off. It's a natural thought."

"So now you're sure he's heading for Mexico."

"I didn't say that. I said that's where I would go if I was on the run."

"Well, your word is good enough for me," she said.

"It's not my *word* we'd be going by," he said. "It's my instinct."

"Lawman's instinct?"

He looked at her sharply and then said, "Old lawman's instinct, yes."

She grinned at him and moved over to his side of the fire, close to him.

"You're not so old."

"I'm a lot older than you," he said, remembering her confession to being twenty-five.

"Pooh," she said, "fifteen years or so."

"Or so," he agreed.

She slid her hand inside his shirt to rub his chest, and said, "That didn't bother you before."

"When you do that," he told her, "it doesn't bother me now, either."

"What about when I do this?" she asked. She got to her knees and put her mouth on his, forcing her tongue between his lips.

"That's even better," he said.

It was a warm night—although there was a cool breeze—and their clothes came off very easily and naturally. Clint spread a blanket out and then eased Anne down onto it.

"Don't play," she whispered, "let's just do it. I'm ready."

He felt between her legs and found that she *was* slickly ready. Her raised himself over her, and his hard member slid into her as if it belonged there.

As if she could read his mind, she said, "Oh God, yes, it belongs there."

He began to take her in long, slow strokes and she tightened her arms around him and eventually lifted her legs and wrapped them around him. The unyielding ground beneath them made for maximum penetration, which she seemed to appreciate very much, judging from the sounds she was making in his ear.

"Oh yes," she whispered during a fairly lucid moment. "Oh Clint, yes, keep doing it, don't ever stop."

"Everything's got to stop sometime, Anne," he said, kissing her neck.

"Not this, oh please, not this," she moaned. "Don't ever let this stop."

He continued taking her in long, deep strokes, but the tempo was increasing of its own accord and soon he was pounding into her without regard for what the hard ground must be doing to her backside. Up to that point, however, she wasn't complaining, and her moans and sighs continued to be ones of pleasure, not of pain.

Suddenly the moon came out full, and that seemed to be the signal for their mutual orgasms. She cried aloud when she came, and he emitted a suppressed groan of release. She stayed as she was, with him growing soft inside her, and the moon disappeared as suddenly as it had appeared.

"There's only one thing I love more than feeling you go soft inside me," she said.

"What's that?"

"Feeling you get hard."

She ran her hands down over the line of his back to his buttocks, where she began probing and stroking.

"You keep that up, and that's exactly what you're going to get," he said into her ear.

She laughed happily and said, "I know."

After they had dressed and were sitting around the fire again with coffee, Clint realized what a foolish thing they had done. True, he'd neither seen nor heard any sign of Dirk White and his friends, but that didn't mean they weren't there. Anyone could have walked right into their camp while they were on that blanket.

"It was as much my fault as it was yours," she said, studying his face.

"Hmm?"

She inclined her head toward the blanket, which they had not rolled up after they finished.

"What are you, a mind reader?"

"No, just a lucky guess. Anybody could have walked up to us while we were . . . occupied."

"That's what I was thinking," he confirmed.

"I'm sorry, then, but I couldn't help it. Riding with you for so long, and not . . . being with you. I just couldn't wait anymore."

"We'll have to make this time last us—at least until we've finished what we started."

"All right," she said contritely. "If you can do it, I can."

"Thanks a lot."

"For what?"

"That puts all the pressure on me, and as I've told you many times before, you're just too damned beautiful for your own good."

"Keep telling me," she said.

"You've been told that before, haven't you?"

"Not the way you say it."

"How's that?"

"You're not after anything when you say it. You say it because you mean it."

"I always say what I mean, Anne."

"I know," she said.

In the next town, Carson, there was a telegraph message waiting for Clint—who had been careful to tell his friends *not* to use his real name, so the message was waiting for "Duke." The telegraph operator was quite surprised when Duke turned out to be a pretty woman.

"My father wanted a boy," Anne told him, and hurriedly left town with the telegram.

When she reached camp she was waving the telegram over her head, and then she dismounted and handed it to Clint.

"Did you read it?"

"Would I read your mail?" she asked with an innocent look.

"You read it," he said, unfolding it.

"It confirms what you said last night, Clint," she said impatiently. "He's heading for Mexico."

Clint read the message, which was from Rick Hartman in Labyrinth, and that was what it said, all right.

"We've got to get there ahead of him."

He folded the telegram and put it in his pocket thoughtfully.

"What's wrong?"

He scratched his head, looking sheepish.

"Well, after all my talk about shortcuts, I can't think of one across Texas to Mexico."

"Well, I can," Anne said.

"Oh really?"

"Yes. We've got two fine horses, Clint," she said. "We'll just have to ride like hell."

TWENTY-TWO

Katy Little Flower's fine Indian pony was hard put to match strides with the gigantic gelding, Duke, and Clint was careful not to let the big black outdistance the smaller pony and its rider.

They bypassed Labyrinth—which was in itself a shortcut, since it would have been difficult for Clint to simply pass through the town that had almost become home to him—and continued on until they reached a small border town called Rio Rojo.

"We've got to rest these animals," Clint said as they rode into town.

"Do you think we got here first?"

"I don't think we'll know that for a while," Clint said. "We traveled in a straight line, but there's no guarantee that he intends—or intended—to cross here."

"We busted our tails—"

"Our horse's tails," Clint corrected, patting Duke's lathered neck.

"Somebody's tails," she said in frustration, "and we don't even know if it did any good."

"It did some good," Clint said as they pulled to a halt in front of a small livery.

"What good?" she demanded, daring him to come up with something.

"He certainly had no reason to push his horse as hard as we pushed ours," Clint explained. "At the very least, we had to close some ground on him."

"Still," Anne said, grudgingly, "we won't know how much for a while."

"Patience, Annie," Clint said. "If you learn anything from this, learn that."

"Yeah."

They each cared for their horses themselves, and when that was done they went to the small town's only hotel to register.

"We only got one room left," the old Mexican clerk told them.

"We'll muddle through," Clint said. "You have bath facilities?"

The old man began to laugh so hard that he dissolved into a wheezing cough. When he recovered from that he said, "*Sí*, we got a horse trough out back."

"Thanks. Can we get a couple of buckets of water and a basin?"

The old man nodded, still chuckling, and said, "I will tend to it, Señor, Señora."

They didn't bother to correct him.

The adobe hotel was so small that all of the rooms were on one floor—the main floor.

"Can you imagine this dump being filled up?" she asked when they reached their room.

"Did you notice how many rooms this place has?"

THE BOUNTY WOMEN

"Who cares?" she said, flopping down on the bed.

"Anne, can I say something?"

"Go ahead," she said, with her arm thrown across her eyes.

"I sense a growing . . . change of attitude in you."

She moved her arm away from her eyes and stared at him for a few seconds before replying.

"Not a change of attitude, Clint," she said. "I'm just dog-tired."

"So am I. Want to call it off?"

"No!" she snapped, sitting upright. "I want Wallmann more than ever now—I just wish he'd stop and wait for us somewhere so we could get it over with."

"He's not about to do that, so get some rest and we'll get on our way again in a little while, as soon as the horses have had enough of a breather."

"Where are you going?"

"I'm going to walk around and ask some questions."

"That won't take very long. Town's no bigger than a fingernail, and there can't be more than three people in it."

"Just relax and I'll be back in a while."

"I'm just gonna take a . . . little . . . nap . . ." Anne said, and was asleep before Clint left the room.

Clint found the saloon, which was a small wood-plank bar in a tiny general store, and ordered a beer.

"You want it cold?" the bartender asked.

"If you've got it," Clint said, surprised.

"I ain't."

"Then I'll take what you've got."

"You got it."

The man, a tall, slim Texan by all appearances, brought Clint a lukewarm beer in a glass mug.

"At least it's wet," the man said.

"That'll have to do," Clint said, drinking half of it. He hated warm beer, but it cut the dust.

"This place yours?"

"Every blessed inch of it," the man said, "which ain't a whole hell of a lot. You lookin' to buy?"

"Can't oblige you there, friend, but maybe you can help me out."

"I'll try."

"I'm looking for Bill Wallmann," Clint said, deciding to get right to the point. If Wallmann had passed through this hole in the ground, he couldn't have gone unnoticed.

"Wallmann."

"You know who he is?"

"Oh yeah, I know who he is. I seen him not two days ago, standing right where you're standing."

"Two days?" Clint asked. They had indeed made up time on Wallmann, considering how far behind him they had been when they'd left Dry Creek.

"You after the price on his head?" the man asked.

Clint shook his head.

"I'm just trying to keep somebody alive, friend. Did he go on across the border?"

"Said he was going to. Said he needed some time, and Mexico was the only place he could get it. Guess you ain't gonna give it to him, huh?"

"I wish I could," Clint said. "I really wish I could, but it's not mine to give." He finished his drink and said, "Thanks for the beer—and the information."

"Mind some advice?"

Clint stopped short and turned back to the man.

"Go ahead."

"Wallmann's always been dangerous, from what I

hear," the man said, "but there's something else inside of him now."

"What?"

The bartender shrugged. "Meanness, maybe, I don't know. Kept rubbing his head, too, like it hurt him all the time. Made him edgy. I don't need to tell you what an edgy gunman is like."

Clint frowned and said, "Why don't you have to tell me?"

"Hell, I seen the Gunsmith in action twice, myself," the bartender said, "both times in Texas. I know you're good, Adams, but Wallmann is . . . edgy. That means you ain't gonna be able to predict what he's gonna do. You know what I'm talking about?"

"Yeah, I do," Clint said, frowning at the man. "What's your name, friend?"

"That don't matter none," the bartender answered. "Let's just say I was a hand with a gun once, and this is where I ran to. Wallmann's running a little further, and he ain't gonna like anybody following him. Take my advice, Adams. You find him, you better just shoot him in the back and be done with it."

"Thanks for the advice, friend," Clint said, "but I've never shot a man who wasn't facing me, and I don't intend to start now."

"Then you better be as good as your reputation says you are. I seen your move twice, and I don't think you can take Wallmann face to face."

"I'll let you know what happens," Clint said, "on my way back this way."

Clint went back to the hotel and watched Anne sleep for two hours before waking her.

"Time to get going."

"Have the horses rested enough?" she asked, knuckling her eyes in an attempt to clear them.

"Enough to walk, and that's all they have to do."

"Why?" she asked, pushing herself to a sitting position and looking at him anxiously. "How far behind him are we?"

"Two days."

"Two days?"

"And he's going to get where he's going pretty soon. It won't be long now, Annie. Just be a little more patient."

She thought about it for a while, then made fists against the mattress and pushed herself to a standing position.

"Let's go get the sonofabitch!"

Clint Adams had crossed the Rio Grande many times over the years, but it had never felt quite as cold as it did that day.

TWENTY-THREE

Bill Wallmann had reached his destination the previous day, a town called Palo Negro. He had taken a room in the town's small, two-story hotel—overlooking the main street—then had purchased a bottle of whiskey and taken it to his room with him.

He was finished running, and he pitied anyone who didn't leave him alone and let him sort things out.

Pedro Montalban considered himself an opportunistic man. When an opportunity presented itself to him, he reached out with both hands and grabbed hold and he did not let go until he had wrung everything out of it that he could.

Pedro had seen the stranger ride into town, had watched him go to the hotel, then to the cantina and then back to the hotel with a bottle.

He knew who the man was.

He called together his friends Carlos Perez, Pascal

Torres and Felix Mantilla, and brought them to the cantina to talk over this newest opportunity.

"Do you all know who Bill Wallmann is?"

The three men exchanged glances and Mantilla said, "Is that not the *gringo* gunman?"

"It is. He is here in town."

"So?" Perez asked. He was the dimwitted one of the group, and the others very often ignored anything he had to say. He was also very deadly with a knife, which was why they kept him around.

"The *gringo* has a price on his head, *amigos*, a very high price."

"How much?" Torres asked with interest.

"Six thousand American dollars."

"That is *mucho dinero*," Mantilla agreed.

"Divided four ways it is still much money," Montalban reminded them.

"*Sî*," Torres agreed.

"What must we do for this money?" Perez asked.

"A very good question, Carlos."

"And do you have a very good answer, Pedro?" Perez asked, in what he thought was a great display of wit.

"Yes, I do, Carlos," Montalban said. "We must kill him."

"How will we collect the money, Pedro?" Torres asked. "He has crossed the border and is no longer in his own country."

"Simplicity itself," Montalban said with a wide, gold-toothed smile. "We must kill him, then take him across the border. No one must know that he was killed here. Bounty hunters do it all the time."

"Are we to become bounty hunters, Pedro?" Perez asked.

"Carlos, my friend," Pedro said, "we are to become rich."

Looking excited, the dim-witted Perez asked, "When we split the money four ways, how much will I get?"

"That is simple, Carlos," Montalban said, exchanging glances with the other two men. "You will get all for yourself five hundred American dollars."

"Five hundred?" Perez repeated eagerly. He looked at his three friends, who all nodded, and Perez said, "We will *all* be rich with such a sum!"

"Yes," Pedro Montalban said, "we will."

TWENTY-FOUR

"I've never been to Mexico before," Anne Archer said.

"Well, look around you, because this is it."

There wasn't very much to see at the moment, just trees and mesquite and rocks, but Clint had assured her that very soon they would be coming to a town.

"What's this town called again?"

"Paso Infierno. It means Gateway to Hell," he said.

"Why would anyone call a town that?"

"Because when you say it in Spanish it sounds so pretty."

"Clint?"

"Yes?"

"When we catch up to Wallmann, how are we going to . . . to take him?"

"I don't know."

"What about what that man said in Rio Rojo."

He looked at her sharply and said, "You don't mean about shooting him in the back, do you?"

"Uh, no . . ." she said, keeping her voice low, obviously sorry she had brought it up.

He didn't choose to pursue the matter, and they rode the remainder of the way to Paso Infierno in silence.

As they reached the town she said, "Clint, I'm sorry."

"Forget it."

"I just didn't realize that it was such a sore point with you," she said. "I'm really sorry."

"It's all right, Anne." How could she know that his one great fear in life was of being shot in the back, the way Bill Hickok had been. That was no way for a man to die—*any* man, no matter who he was. "I shouldn't be that sensitive about it. It's just not something I would ever do."

"I realize that."

"Let's get the horses taken care of, and then we can check around and see if Wallmann passed through here."

"You're going to ask?"

"Yes. I don't think we have to worry anymore. Wallmann has probably reached wherever he was headed. Even if he knows we're coming—or anybody else—he'll dig in and stay put."

"What about your friend?"

"Jake Benteen?" Clint asked. "He's not exactly my friend, but I've wondered about that myself."

After the horses were taken care of, Clint sent Anne over to the cantina while he checked in with the local law.

"Sheriff?" he said to the man behind the desk in the sheriff's office.

"That's right," the man said, standing up so that Clint could see that he wore a sheriff's badge on his chest, and was not a deputy. "What can I do for you?"

The man looked like a tired forty, with lines and creases all over his face and a resigned slump to his shoulders. Clint had a hunch that if the man had to be a sheriff, he was in the right town for it.

"I'm looking for Bill Wallmann."

"Is that a fact?"

"Yes. Have you seen him?"

"Can't say as I have," the sheriff replied, and then added, "but he was here."

"He was?"

"Couple of days ago. Stayed in his hotel and didn't cause any trouble. I didn't have any reason to see him."

Clint could see that the sheriff was very relieved about that.

"How long did he stay?"

"A day. He left the next morning."

"Anybody talk to him?"

"Hell, no. The man might have had the plague, the way everybody kept out of his way."

Clint nodded. Wallmann was the kind of man who did not invite familiarity.

"Well, thanks for your time, Sheriff."

"Sure. You gonna take him in?"

"I'm going to try."

"You law? This is Mexico, you know, not the United States."

"That big body of water I crossed," Clint said, "that was the Rio Grande?"

The sheriff frowned, as if wondering if Clint was kidding him, then decided that he was.

"I was just telling you."

"Thanks. I appreciate it."

"You gonna stay in town long?"

"Just long enough to get something to eat and rest our horses."

"Horses?"

"Mine and my partner's."

"Who's your partner?"

"Why all the questions?" Clint asked suddenly.

The man took a step back and said, "Well, I *am* the sheriff."

"Why don't you just go back to doing your job the way you were when I walked in?"

The sheriff frowned at Clint's tone of voice and said, "Well . . . sure, mister, sure."

"Just treat me the way you treated Wallmann, and we'll get along fine."

As Clint left, the sheriff stared after him and decided that was just the way he *should* treat this stranger.

Clint went to the cantina, where Anne was seated alone at a table with a beer. She was being looked over by a couple of Mexicans at one of the other two tables in the place. He got himself a beer and sat with her, and the two Mexicans suddenly found their boots more interesting.

"They bother you?"

"No. If they did, I'd handle it. What'd you find out from the sheriff?"

"Wallmann came through here, stayed one night and pulled out."

"When?"

"Couple of days ago."

"We're close."

"And getting closer. I have a feeling this will all be over soon, Anne. Very soon."

"The sooner the better."

Those were his sentiments exactly.

They stayed in the cantina just long enough to give the horses some rest, and then left Paso Infierno and continued on. From that point on, every town they came to could be the town where Wallmann had stopped. Clint's "old lawman's instincts" were going to have to be working overtime.

TWENTY-FIVE

Carlos Perez made the mistake of thinking that five hundred American dollars was all the money in the world. He thought that Pedro and the others were being too careful of this American gunman. Carlos was not frightened by the man's reputation. He also knew that he was faster with his knife than any man could be with a gun.

They had been taking turns keeping an eye on the American, Wallmann, and now it was Carlos's turn. He had watched Wallmann enter the cantina a few hours earlier, and now the man came out, carrying a bottle in his hand. From the way he walked, it was obvious that he was drunk.

This was Carlos's chance to show Pedro and the others that he wasn't as dumb as they thought he was.

As Wallmann started down the street toward the hotel, Carlos crossed over and followed. At that point his relief arrived and saw him. Felix Mantilla thought he knew what was on Perez's mind, and he went to find Pedro Montalban and Pascal Torres.

They wouldn't want to miss this.

Wallmann knew he was being followed. He could feel it—and he felt sorry for the man, because he had a headache that was getting worse. All he wanted was to go to his room and go to sleep. If the man tried to keep him from doing that . . .

"Should we try and stop him?" Pascal Torres asked when Felix Mantilla told him and Montalban what he thought Carlos Perez was up to.

"No," Montalban said, getting to his feet. "Let's go and watch our friend Carlos in action. If he kills Wallmann, that will suit our purpose, and if he doesn't"—Montalban shrugged— "a three-way split is better than a four-way split."

"We were only going to give him five hundred anyway," Mantilla said.

"Still," Montalban said, "an extra five hundred is an extra five hundred—and our friend Carlos really is very good with his knives, is he not?"

"He is the best—but against a gun?" Mantilla said.

"I've seen him throw his knife *through* a man before the man could touch his gun," Torres said.

"But a man like Bill Wallmann?" Mantilla asked.

"If we don't hurry," Montalban said, "we won't be there to find out."

When they got outside, Carlos Perez had already called out to Bill Wallmann and they were facing each other.

"You are a wanted man, Señor," Perez said.
"Not in Mexico."

"I will take you back to the United States."

"Alive?"

"That is up to you, Señor," Perez said, enjoying himself. Maybe he would go into the bounty-hunting business.

"Mister," Wallmann said, squinting his eyes against the pain in his head, "you're keeping me from something very important."

"Like what?" Perez asked, curiously.

"A nap," Wallmann said. "A nap that could keep you alive."

Perez had one of his throwing knives in his hand, holding it down at his side against his leg. He had no way of knowing that Bill Wallmann's sharp eyes had picked it up long ago.

"You are making a joke, Señor," Perez said. "Please take out your gun and drop it to the ground."

Wallmann shook his head and said, "Not a chance."

There were not many men who could flip a knife underhand and hit a target, but Carlos Perez had practiced and practiced until he was an expert. Most men expected a blade man to reach back and throw a knife overhand. Many men had stared in awe at Carlos after his knife had buried itself in their guts as the result of an underhand flip.

"You force my hand, Señor," Carlos Perez said to Wallmann.

"And you mine."

Wallmann was annoyed now. He watched the Mexican carefully, and when he saw the muscles of Perez's right arm tighten, he drew his gun and fired.

The bullet punched Carlos Perez in the chest, driving the air from his lungs. The fingers of his right hand opened and his knife fell harmlessly to the ground as he stared at

Wallmann in awe and wonder.

As Perez died, Pedro Montalban said, "I guess Carlos wasn't as good as he thought."

The other two men weren't listening. They too were staring in awe at Wallmann, who had turned his back and was walking to his hotel.

Pedro Montalban had a feeling that this would become less than a three-way split before it was over.

Wallmann went back to his hotel room knowing that news of what had happened would get around, and if there wasn't someone already after him, there soon would be.

TWENTY-SIX

Word reached Clint and Anne in the town just before Palo Negro.

"That means he's less than a couple of miles from here," Anne said excitedly. "Let's go."

They were sitting in the cantina, where they had heard the news from the bartender, who was telling everyone he could.

"Simmer down," Clint said, putting his hand on her arm. "Before we go rushing in, we've got to know exactly what we're going to do."

"We're going to take him in!"

"Sure, but if he happens to spot us as we're riding in, he's going to recognize us. He's seen us both before, you know."

"That's right. What are we going to do?"

"We're going to stay here until a couple of hours before dark, then we'll ride to Palo Negro, and after darkness comes, we'll ride in. By morning we'll already be there, probably without his knowledge."

"And then what?"

"And then we wait for our chance to take him . . . alive."

She thought about it and then said, "I guess it's as good a plan as any."

"I've got another plan too," he said in a softer tone.

"Oh? Is it better than the last one?"

"Much better," he said, standing up and taking her hand.

She was sitting on top of him, grinding the fine hairs of her pubic bush down against his wiry ones, taking him as deeply as he would go. Her head was throw back and her breath was coming in great gulps.

He reached for her and pulled her down until she was lying on him, full length. He cupped her firm buttocks, kneading them as they moved together with one tempo, driving each other to completion.

Afterward, while she was lying in his arms, she said, "It's almost over now, Clint."

"Yes, it is."

"What will you do then?"

"Move on, I guess," he said. "Collect my rig and move on."

"Alone?"

He looked down at her and she said quickly, "Forget I said that."

"No, I won't forget it—but I will be going alone, Anne. I'm sorry, but—"

"You don't owe me any explanations," she said.

"I can explain—"

"No, I don't want you to. I just want *you* to know that *I* won't be saying good-bye."

He squeezed her in his arms and said, "Nobody said

anything about saying good-bye. The West isn't all that big."

"No, I guess it isn't."

He propped himself up on one elbow and looked down at her compellingly lovely face. If he *could* stay with one woman, he thought . . . No, that wasn't in the cards for him, his past was proof of that. He might as well enjoy her now—they might as well enjoy *each other* now—while they were still together.

He kissed her eyes and then her mouth, and then continued on to her neck, her belly, until his nose was nestled among those fine hairs between her legs.

"Oh God—" she said, lifting her hips to the pressure of his tongue, "make it last, please, make it last until next time."

Of course, they both knew that in going after Bill Wallmann there was always a chance that there wouldn't be a next time—for either one of them.

TWENTY-SEVEN

"It's time," Clint said, shaking her awake.

"I'm ready."

They were camped just outside Palo Negro, and Anne had fallen asleep lying against Clint's shoulder. Now it was time to ride into town under cover of darkness, avoiding, if possible, the notice of Wallmann.

As they rode she asked, "Clint, how good is Wallmann with a gun?"

"You've seen him."

"When I entered the cabin his gun was already out," she reminded him. "How fast is he, really?"

"He's fast."

"As fast as you?"

"I don't know."

"How fast was Hickok? You and he were friends, weren't you?"

"Yes, we were," Clint said. "Bill was faster than God, if God wore a gun."

"Was *he* faster than you?"

Clint didn't like speculation about who was faster, him or Hickok. Neither one of them had ever gone to the bother of finding out, and he told Anne that.

"I'm sorry," she said. "I'm nervous, and I guess I'm talking too much about the wrong things."

"It's all right," he said, realizing that by answering her he'd be keeping her mind off what was going to happen. "When people talk about who was fastest with a gun, I guess I have the honor of being mentioned in the same breath with Bill, but I've heard Wallmann mentioned that way as well. Bill set the standard, I think, that all men with a rep are measured by. Wes Hardin, Bat Masterson, Bill Longley, Murphy the Irish Gun, they all get mentioned, but Bill is always the name that comes first."

"You've beaten some fast guns in your time," she said.

"It's not something I'm proud of," he said, "nor is it something I'm ashamed of. Yes, I've outdrawn some fast men, but only when I had no other choice."

"I've heard of some of the men you've . . . beaten," she said, deciding not to use the word *killed*. "Kid Dragon, Dale Leighton, Stansfield Lloyd, Big John Stud—the list is long and impressive."

Clint wouldn't have discussed this with anyone else, but she seemed to need this. Maybe her confidence was wavering, and she needed to convince herself that she was standing with a living legend.

"They were all good men with a gun, all right."

"But you were better."

"On that particular day when we met, I was better, yes. The line between all of us is thin, I think, Anne. If we had met on another day, who knows what would have happened?"

THE BOUNTY WOMEN

"Well then, we have to hope that when it comes down to you—us—and Wallmann, it'll be our day."

"I suppose so."

"Have you known many women who were fast with a gun?" she asked suddenly.

"Not that I can recall," he said. "Lacy Blake is pretty good, accurate, but I can't say she's that fast."

"I'm good," she said. "I hit what I aim at, but I don't know if I'm especially fast."

"Let's hope you never have to find out," he said. That wasn't exactly a boost to her confidence, but Clint truthfully felt that way. He didn't want Anne testing herself to see how fast she was, not against the likes of Bill Wallmann.

Clint didn't know for sure how he'd fare against Wallmann, but one thing he did know was that Anne Archer wouldn't have a prayer. The last thing he wanted to do was make her think she did, just to make her feel confident.

All that would do was get her killed.

TWENTY-EIGHT

They rode into Palo Negro and found very few lights on in the town. The cantina was lit, but there wasn't much sound coming from it. Clint had an impression of a sleepy little Mexican town that retired early.

They found the livery, and although no one was around, it wasn't locked.

"They've either got good law hereabouts," he told Anne, "or a lot of trust."

"Maybe they just don't care."

"That too. Come on, we'll put the horses up ourselves."

They took care of that and then discussed their next move.

"This town is bound to have one hotel," he said, "and if we go over there we might bump into Wallmann before we're ready."

"The same goes for the cantina," she said.

"Right. I think what we're going to have to do is—"

He stopped short as something occurred to him, and he tried it out on her.

"I think maybe *you* should stay right here in the livery."

"What about you?"

"Well, Wallmann has seen you with Sandy and Katy Little Flower. He knows you're after him, but he doesn't know that I am. He knows me, but when he sees me he's not going to jump to any conclusions. He might think that I'm just passing through."

"And if he doesn't?"

"Then this thing'll end faster than we thought," Clint said. "I think I'm going to go over to the cantina. If he's there I can act surprised and talk to him."

"You're still not convinced, are you?" Anne asked.

"About what?"

"That he's changed. That he's become a vicious killer."

"Killing was always just a job for Wallmann," Clint said, "a way to make a living. He didn't like it, it was just what he did best. I guess maybe I need a little convincing that he's changed, yeah."

"What about what he did to Sandy and Katy?"

"That could go under the heading of self-preservation, Anne."

She tightened her lips, but didn't argue further with him.

"All right," she said, "go ahead, go find out for yourself. I'll stay hidden here."

"I'll be back," he told her, touching her shoulder.

"You better be."

Clint left the shelter of the livery and started toward the lighted cantina. When he reached it he peered in through a window first and saw that the place was about half-

THE BOUNTY WOMEN

full—which meant there were about five people inside. He stepped through the batwing doors and approached the bar.

"*Qué pasa, Señor?*" the bartender asked. "What can I get for you?"

"A beer," he said, "cold if you have it, but I'm not counting on it."

"Very wise, Señor," the bartender said, smiling broadly.

Clint took his beer and examined the room from the corner of his eye. There were exactly five men present, and from the looks of things, they were all together. One of them was doing all the talking in a low voice, and from time to time Clint could see a glint of gold in the man's mouth. He'd never understand the attraction gold teeth had for Mexicans. He could think of a lot better things to do with gold.

The five men were playing cards, but it seemed as if they were doing it simply to pass the time.

"Señor," the bartender said in a low voice, "a little advice."

Clint looked at the man and said, "Go ahead, amigo. I'm listening."

"Do not think of joining them in their poker game, Señor," he said. "Those are very bad men."

"Is that right?"

"*Sí*, Señor, especially the one doing all the talking, with the gold teeth? That is Pedro Montalban."

"I never heard of him."

"Perhaps not, but in Mexico he has a—how you say—*reputación*."

"Reputation."

"*Sí*. Also, he has lost a friend in the past couple of days."

"Oh? How?"

"He was killed by a *gringo*—excuse me, an American such as yourself, Señor."

"What's his name?"

"Wallmann, Bill Wallmann." Up to that point the man's accent had not been too bad, but he pronounced Wallmann's first name "Beel." "You have heard of him, no?"

"I have heard of him, yes."

"Pedro has vowed revenge, he and other friends of poor Carlos. That is what they are talking about now."

"I see. Tell me, is this Pedro likely to face Bill Wallmann in the street?"

The man snorted disgustedly and said, "Pedro Montalban has a *reputación*, Señor—for shooting people in the back! That is probably how he will kill the *gringo*—uh, the American."

"In the back," Clint said, feeling a chill. Complications had set in, then. He doubted that this Pedro Montalban was simply looking for revenge. More than likely he was looking for the bounty on Wallmann's head, and the man would not take kindly to Clint and Anne's walking off with it. Also, Clint would not be able to stand by and watch a man like Wallmann get shot in the back.

Complications had definitely set in, because if he and Anne wanted to take Wallmann, there would be opposition—and not just from Wallmann himself!

"Okay," Clint said when he returned to the livery, "I've got a new plan."

"What did you find out?"

Briefly he told her what he'd found out in the cantina, that Wallmann was here, and that he had managed to make some dangerous enemies already.

THE BOUNTY WOMEN 141

"But if we leave it to them, they'll do the job for us?" Anne said. "Won't they?"

"You wouldn't get the money, Anne," Clint pointed out, "and besides, I can't stand by and watch Wallmann get shot, not in the back."

"What is this thing you have about not shooting people in the back? Somebody else would be doing it, wouldn't they?"

"That's not the point," he said. "Hickok was shot in the back. When the time comes for me to get mine, it will probably be in the back too. I may not be able to prevent that, but I sure as hell am going to prevent anyone else from dying that way. It's a hell of a way for anyone to die, Anne!"

She could see by his eyes that he was really upset over this thing. She knew now that if the legendary Gunsmith was afraid of anything, it was of getting shot in the back. Maybe she could convince him that what he needed was someone to ride with him and watch his back.

Maybe later.

"All right," she said, "we'll do it your way. What's your new plan?"

"I'm going over to the hotel to register. You sneak around to the back and wait, and when I get a room I'll let you in."

"Then what?"

"Then you'll have to stay in the room while I 'accidentally' run into Wallmann."

"I still have my doubts about him believing that."

"We'll just have to see. I'll see you behind the hotel."

"All right."

When they were in the small room, Anne sat on the bed and asked, "Where's Wallmann's room?"

"He's on the second floor," Clint said. His room was on the main floor.

"Where will you have your meeting with him?"

"At breakfast, I guess," he answered.

"And in the meantime?"

"In the meantime we'd better go to bed," he said, and when he saw the look on her face he added, "to sleep. We're going to need all the rest we can get."

"Yes sir," she said, but as it turned out they didn't go right to sleep, after all.

TWENTY-NINE

In the morning Clint left Anne in the hotel room with a promise to bring her something to eat. He went down to the desk clerk and asked where he could get a good breakfast. The man gave him directions to a small cafe. Clint went there to eat, hoping to see Wallmann, but had no such luck. He asked the waitress to give him something he could take with him, and then smuggled it up to his room for Anne.

"Tortillas for breakfast?" she asked.

"It was something I could carry with me," he said, shrugging.

"Never mind. I'm hungry enough to eat it. Did you see him?"

"No, if he had breakfast he had it somewhere else."

"And if he didn't?"

"He's either going to have it later or not at all. There's a possibility that he stays in his room most of the time."

"Then we'd have to go in and get him."

"I don't think so. He's got to come out sometime."

"And we just wait?"

"We've been patient this long," Clint said. "Why not a little longer?"

She made a face, but didn't argue.

"That talkative bartender at the cantina might be able to tell me a little more about what kind of routine he's been following," he said, getting up.

"You're going to have a drink now? This early?"

"Look who's talking," he said. "A woman who eats tortillas for breakfast."

She would have thrown the second tortilla at him, but she was too hungry to waste it.

Clint walked to the cantina, not expecting to find it open, but it was. He entered and found that no one was present but the bartender.

"Ah, good morning, Señor," the bartender greeted him. "You would like a—uh, how you Americans say—a morning pick-you-up?"

"Some conversation, perhaps," Clint said. "What is your name?"

"I am called Chico, Señor. It is not my full name, but that is how I am called. How are you called, Señor? I must know, if we are to be *amigos*."

"I am Clint."

"*Con mucho gusto*," Chico said, sticking out a meaty hand. "What is it I can tell you?"

"It's about Bill Wallmann."

"*Sî?*"

"Is he staying in the hotel?"

"Oh, *sî*, Señor. He not only stays there, he *stays* there."

"How do you mean?"

"The only time he comes out is to come over here to get some more whiskey."

"You mean he's living on whiskey? No food?"

"I have not personally seen him eat anything, Señor. And my cousin, who runs the cafe, he has not ever seen him in there—and who would eat anywhere else? My cousin's wife is a wonderful cook—"

"I know, Chico, I ate there myself this morning."

"Ah, *bueno*—"

"How often does he come over for a bottle?"

"Last time he took, uh, two—no, *perdone—uno, dos, tres*—ah, three bottle, and that was, uh—" Touching his fingers, he once again sought the correct English equivalent, and then said, "Ah, two days ago, Señor. He should come back today for some, no?"

"Maybe," Clint said thoughtfully. "Do Pedro Montalban and his friends know about Wallmann's drinking habits?"

"Oh, *sî*, Señor," Chico said, with a grave look on his face. "They have been studying him very carefully. They know," he concluded, nodding his head gravely now.

"I see. Thanks for the information, Chico."

"*Sî, por nada, Señor.*"

Clint started for the door, but stopped when Chico said, "Excuse me, Señor."

"Yes?"

"You do not wish the pick-you-up?"

"Not quite this early, Chico. Maybe later."

"Sî."

He was almost out the door when Chico once again said, *"Perdone, Señor?"*

"Yes?"

"Your curiosity, I cannot help but be curious about it

myself. Why do you have so much interest in this man?"

"He's a fellow American," Clint said.

"Ahh, *sî*," Chico said, as if he understood, but he was scratching his head as Clint left the cantina, because he didn't understand at all. He did not have such an interest in his fellow Mexicans.

He would never understand the *gringos*.

THIRTY

"So?"

"So what?" Clint asked.

"What are you going to do now?"

"I think I'm going to have to spend the entire day in the saloon."

Her eyes widened and she said, "Which means that I have to stay in this hotel room all day—alone?"

"I'm afraid so."

She narrowed her eyes suddenly and said, "Clint, I'm beginning to get a little suspicious here."

"Of what? Of me?"

She nodded and said, "Are you sure you're not just trying to keep me out of trouble?"

"Would I do that? Don't the reasons I gave you for staying in this room make sense?"

She frowned and said, "That's the problem, they do."

"All right, then. Don't worry about being kept out of trouble, Anne. When the trouble starts, you're going to be right there."

"Really?"

"Damn right. I'm going to need your gun."

Clint took up residence at a back table in the cantina. From the bartender he managed to scrounge up a dogeared deck of cards and an occasional mug of lukewarm beer. Customers came and went, eyeing him suspiciously, and he suspected that word had started to circulate that there was a stranger in town who was practically living in the saloon. Of course, since Wallmann rarely came out of his room, he wouldn't be hearing such news, but maybe Pedro Montalban would, and come to investigate.

When Pedro Montalban heard the news about the stranger, he became very interested.

"Why should a stranger interest us?" Mantilla asked.

"Because this stranger just might turn out to be a bounty hunter looking for Bill Wallmann," Montalban said. "Do you want to share the reward with him?"

"No."

They were in the crumbling adobe house that Montalban lived in, and Pedro got up from his bed and said, "Perhaps we had better go over and find out who he is, then. If he is a bounty hunter, we might be able to persuade him to leave town."

It took a few hours, but Montalban finally showed up, with his friends in tow. He went right to the bar, where he held a short conversation with the bartender, and then he and his two friends turned and approached Clint's table. Each of them was carrying a glass of whiskey in the hand that was not his gunhand.

"Señor, do you mind if we join you?"

"Yes."

"*Perdone, Señor?*" Montalban asked, frowning.

"I do mind if you join me."

"You do not wish our company?"

"That's right, I don't."

Montalban exchanged glances with his two friends, and then looked back at Clint.

"My friends are very insulted, Señor, that you do not wish to drink with them."

"Well, why don't you just explain to your friends that it's not them I object to."

Montalban's frown deepened and he said, "Señor?"

"It's you I object to, Montalban."

"Señor, are you trying to insult me?"

"Not that I know of. I simply don't think I would like your company."

Montalban put his drink down on Clint's table with a bang, spilling half of the contents, and backed away, his hand hovering near his gun. His two friends put down their glasses and spread out, keeping their eyes on Montalban.

"Now hold on a minute," Clint said. "If I offended you fellas, I'm sure I'm sorry, but I believe I have the right to drink with whom I please—I mean, even if I am in Mexico." Clint looked at the bartender and said, "Is there some law in this country that says I can't refuse to drink with somebody?"

"Not that I know of, Señor," the bartender answered.

"See?" Clint said, spreading his hands. "No need for anyone to get insulted."

Montalban and his friends were totally confused now. As far as Pedro was concerned, how could he draw on a man who was being so agreeable?

"I am curious about something, Señor."

"What's that?"

"Why you are here."

"Well, I don't really think that's any of your business—not that I'm being insulting," Clint added quickly, holding out his hand. "I don't want you to misunderstand me again."

"Señor, please," Montalban said, "if I may sit a moment?"

Clint made a show of considering the question and then made a suggestion.

"Why don't you send your two friends back to the bar, and then we can have a nice friendly talk, okay?"

Montalban turned and spoke to the other two men in Spanish, and they walked to the bar while he sat down opposite the Gunsmith.

"I am at a disadvantage here, Señor," Montalban said.

"How's that?"

"Señor?"

"How are you at a disadvantage?"

"You know my name and I do not know yours."

"Oh, that's not important."

"I would like to know who you are, Señor."

"No, you wouldn't."

"Señor—"

"You want to know why I'm here."

"*Sí*," Montalban said warily.

"And you want to know if I'm going to mess up your play."

"My . . . play?"

"With Wallmann."

"Ahh, I see. You *are* a bounty hunter."

"No."

"Then you are not interested in Señor Wallmann."

"Yes, I am."

"But you are not a bounty hunter?"

"Right."

"Señor," Montalban said, "I do not like these games that you are playing with me."

What Montalban didn't like was being made to feel stupid ever since he had approached the Gunsmith's table.

"All right then, Montalban, let's quit playing games."

"*Bueno.*"

"You want Wallmann."

"*Sî.*"

"You can't have him."

It was getting so Clint could figure out how confused or upset Montalban was, from the depth of the wrinkles in his brow when he frowned. At the moment he was pretty confused.

"You are not some kind of lawman, are you?" he asked.

"No, I'm not. Even if I was, it wouldn't do me any good in Mexico, would it?"

"No."

"I'm just an hombre who's come a long way to get something done, Montalban, and I won't be very happy if you get in my way."

Now Montalban's brow was a mass of deep wrinkles, and he was getting pretty upset.

"Señor, this is my home, my country, and I have friends here. My friends and I would not be very happy if you got in our way."

"Well, now that we've warned each other—"

"You are warning me?" Montalban asked in disbelief. "You are here alone, Señor. You are not in a position to warn anyone."

"Montalban," Clint said, leaning forward, "I don't need anyone else to help me take care of you and your two clowns over there. Wallmann, he worries me. You and your friends? You don't worry me one bit."

Montalban regarded Clint for several moments in silence, trying to decide whether he was up to something, or was just a crazy American.

"You are not friends with this man, are you?" he asked finally.

"We know each other," Clint said, "but I wouldn't say that we're friends."

"Then I do not understand this," Montalban said, standing up.

Clint smiled and remained silent. Montalban didn't know it, but that was just what the Gunsmith had in mind. He wanted the Mexican so confused he wouldn't be able to concentrate properly on Bill Wallmann.

And judging from the ridges in Montalban's forehead, he'd succeeded.

After Montalban left with his friends—all three of them giving him hard looks, which he assumed were meant to frighten him out of his wits—the bartender came over and said, "A word of advice, Señor?"

"Have I ever refused your advice, Chico?"

"No, Señor, but heed this advice carefully. You have made a dangerous enemy in Pedro Montalban. He would happily cut your throat in your sleep."

"That's all right, Chico," Clint said, rising from his chair. "I'm a pretty dangerous fella myself."

THIRTY-ONE

"You're going to get killed," Anne said, back in the hotel room, "and then where will I be?"

"I'm not going to get killed," he assured her.

"How do you know? If this fellow would cut your throat in your sleep, he wouldn't stop at shooting you in the back, would he?"

"If he shoots me in the back—if he hurts me at all—it might spook Wallmann, and he wants that bounty on Wallmann's head. He's not going to do anything to endanger that."

"You're so sure of yourself."

"It makes sense, Anne, that's all."

"Well, I'm getting cabin fever in here. There must be something I can do."

"There is."

"What?"

"Before leaving the saloon I bought this," he said, showing her the bottle of whiskey he had in his hand.

"I don't want a drink."

"No, but Wallmann does, and you're going to give it to him."

"You're losing me."

"While I was in the saloon I decided to stop waiting for Wallmann to come to us. We're going to go to him."

"By 'us' you mean me, right?"

"Right," he said, extending the bottle toward her. "You and this."

She took the bottle and looked at it dubiously.

"Where are you going to be?"

"Outside his window. When you get his attention, I'll get the drop on him."

She thought it over then nodded and said, "Sounds okay, as long as he doesn't shoot me on sight."

"He won't."

"How can you be so sure?"

"Because you won't have a gun."

"I won't?"

"No, you won't."

"What do I do, hit him with the bottle?"

"That would be a terrible waste of whiskey."

"Wait a minute," she said, sitting down on the bed and putting the fingers of her right hand to her forehead, "let me get this straight. Armed with nothing but a whiskey bottle, I'm supposed to knock on the door of a kill-crazy gunman, and I don't even get to hit him with it?"

"Now you've got the idea."

"I think I was better off staying here in the room."

"Don't worry, I'll be right there."

"He's going to answer the door with his gun in his hand, you know."

"I know, but when he knows it's me behind him, he won't try anything."

"Why not?"

"Because he's a careful man."

"You mean he used to be."

"We'll find out soon enough. Are you ready?"

"We're going to do this now?"

"Right now, before the fog clears from Pedro Montalban's head."

She hefted the whiskey bottle in her hand, then stood up and said, "I'm ready."

"Take off your gunbelt."

She made a face, but put the whiskey bottle down on the bed, undid her gunbelt, hung it on the bedpost, and then picked up the whiskey bottle.

"Now you're ready," Clint said.

Anne stood out in the hall, counting up to twenty-five the way she and Clint had agreed they would do, remembering that the last time she did this she only got as far as twenty. This time, however, she got to twenty-five, which should have meant that Clint was in position. She took a deep breath and knocked on Wallmann's door.

There was no answer.

She knocked again, harder, and again there was no answer.

Her heart was pounding and she decided that this time, if he answered, she was going to let him have it with the bottle and to hell with Clint Adams.

She pounded on the door, and when it opened she brought the bottle back to swing it.

"Hold it! It's me!" Clint shouted, holding his hands out to ward off the blow.

"What—?" she said, gaping at him. She looked past him and saw Wallmann lying on his back, fully dressed on the bed.

"What happened?" she asked.

"Come on in and I'll explain."

She entered the room and he closed the door behind them.

"Did you hit him?" she asked.

"No, I didn't. When I looked in the window he was lying just like that. After you knocked the first time, I thought there might be something wrong with him. I forced the window while you were knocking the second time, and checked on him."

"Is he dead?"

"No, and he's not passed out drunk, either."

"What, then?"

Clint shook his head, looking at the unconscious man on the bed, and said, "I don't know."

"I wonder how long he's been like this."

"From what the bartender told me, he could have been like this for the past two days."

They stood there on either side of the bed, both with puzzled looks on their faces.

"What do we do now?" she asked.

"This isn't right," he said, shaking his head. "A man like Wallmann doesn't let anyone sneak up on him."

"You didn't sneak," Anne said. "You just opened the window and climbed in."

"This isn't right," he said again.

"I'm going to try to wake him," she decided.

"Wait," he said. He bent over and removed Wallmann's gun from its holster, and then said, "Go ahead, give it a try."

She did everything she could, short of sitting on him, but she couldn't wake him.

"God," she said, "it's like he's dead, only he's not."

Clint didn't answer. He bent over the man again and

THE BOUNTY WOMEN

began to examine him closely.

"What are you looking for?"

"A wound."

"What kind of wound?"

"Any kind. Just something that would explain his condition."

"I think we're going to need a doctor for that," Anne said, and Clint looked up at her.

"Good idea," he said. "Since there's no longer any reason for you to stay out of sight, why don't you go and see if you can find one?"

She nodded and started for the door, saying, "I hope this one-horse town has one."

"Don't tell him why you need him, just get him here."

"All right."

After she left, Clint just stood there with Wallmann's gun in his hand, looking down at the man. From all appearances he seemed to be sleeping, but that wasn't the case.

"What the hell is wrong with you?" he asked aloud.

When Anne returned she had a small, gray-haired man in his early fifties with her.

"This is Dr. Estrada."

"What is the problem here?" the doctor demanded of Clint. "The young lady would not explain."

"She couldn't have explained if she wanted to, doctor," Clint said. He gestured toward the bed and said, "We can't wake him up."

The doctor squinted down at the man, then took a pair of wire-framed glasses from his jacket pocket and put them on.

"Who is this man?"

"That's not important right at the moment, doctor," Clint said. "We'd like to know why we can't wake him up."

"I will take a look," the doctor said. He walked to the bed, sat on it, and opened his black bag. Before taking anything out he thumbed open each of Wallmann's eyes, then took a tongue depressor from his bag and forced the man's mouth open. Clint and Anne watched in silence as the doctor continued his examination, which was not unlike the one Clint had given.

"No wounds," the man murmured, and Clint refrained from telling him that they had already established that.

"Anything, doctor?" he said, instead.

The doctor sat there with his jaw in his hand, staring at Wallmann.

"This is very odd."

"What is it?"

"I can only give you an educated guess," the man said, standing up and closing his bag.

"That's better than our own uneducated ones."

"I've done little more than patch up cuts and bruises since I came to this town five years ago. I'm supposed to be retired. If I were you, I would get your friend someplace where they have some modern medicine."

"Doctor, your guess?"

"My guess," the man said, "is that this man is suffering from some kind of pressure here." He tapped his head and said, "The brain is a very fragile thing. The slightest bit of pressure in the right—or wrong—place could cause this kind of reaction."

"What can we do for him?"

"Here? Nothing but wait."

"Wait for what?"

"One of two things," the doctor said. "Either the pressure will subside and he will wake up . . . or he'll simply die."

THIRTY-TWO

Before leaving, the doctor told them that they could throw the man over a horse and take him somewhere else, but that he might be dead by the time they got there.

"My advice is to wait, and if he wakes up, get him someplace where they can care for him properly. If he dies . . ."

So, after the doctor left, they sat on the bed on either side of Wallmann—presenting a ludicrous picture—and discussed their options.

"It's up to you, Anne," Clint said finally. "You and your friends want him dead—"

"Not like this," she said, interrupting him. "I'm not going to toss him over a saddle, hoping he'll die before we get where we're going."

"So what do you want to do?"

"What *can* we do? We'll wait. If he dies here, fine. We'll tie him to the back of a horse and take him out. If he wakes up, we've got his gun. We'll put him up on a horse and take him out that way." She looked at him then and said, "What do you think?"

"I think you're right."

"You do?"

"Yes. We've got only one other problem."

"What's that?"

"We've got to keep Pedro Montalban and his friends from taking him away from us."

"I thought you had him befuddled?"

"That's a good word," Clint said. "I do have him befuddled, but we don't know how long that's going to last, or how long this"—he indicated the unconscious Wallmann—"will last."

"So what do we do?"

"I've got that figured out."

"You have? Already?"

"Sure."

"Tell me."

"We barricade ourselves in here with Wallmann until . . . his situation resolves itself."

"And then what?"

"That part," Clint said, "I don't have figured out yet."

THIRTY-THREE

Once again Clint sent Anne out while he stayed with Wallmann. Montalban couldn't have discovered yet that Anne was with Clint, if he had even spotted her at all. She had gone out to pick up some supplies—food, ammunition, whatever they'd need to hold Wallmann's room safe from Montalban and his boys. When she returned with a burlap bag over her shoulder, Clint went to his room to get their rifles and Anne's gun, as well as their saddlebags.

"Did you get everything?" she asked when he returned.

"Yes, dear," he said, like a dutiful husband, "I got everything."

She stuck her tongue out at him and said, "If we're going to be stuck here together for a while, I'd like to go and take a bath."

"Actually," he said, "it won't be quite that bad. One of us will have to be with him at all times, in case he wakes up, or in case Montalban and company try something."

"If that's the case, then I'm going to go and take a bath."

"You can't."

"Why not?"

"Because you're not registered in the hotel. Bath facilities are for guests only."

"In this dump? If I offer the clerk two bits, he'll jump on it."

"Listen," he said, catching her before she went out the door, "after your bath, go back to my room, and then come up here the back way."

"Sure. Don't go away while I'm gone."

"We'll be here."

When Anne came back, she looked clean and smelled good enough for Clint to wish that Wallmann wasn't on the bed.

"Still here? Any change?" she asked.

"No. Listen, I've got to go back to the room and get another chair—that is, unless you want to keep sitting on the bed with Sleeping Beauty."

"No thanks. Go and get that chair."

"Will you be all right?"

She strapped on her gun, patted it and said, "I'll be fine."

"Okay."

Clint left the room and went downstairs to his room to get a chair. As he passed the clerk, the man gave him a knowing look, and Clint simply winked back. Men of the world.

He went back to his room, grabbed a chair and then brought it up to Wallmann's room by using the back stairs. For all the clerk knew, he and Anne were holed up in his room, and if Montalban came by and paid for information, that's what he'd get.

"Back so soon?" Anne said as he reentered the room. "We didn't even have a chance to get started."

She was nervous, and her attempt at humor was betraying that fact.

"I could go out and come in again in about an hour," he offered.

"That's all right. I don't think I could have gotten much out of him anyway."

"His hard luck."

Clint walked to the bed to look down at Wallmann, and had a weird thought.

"Wouldn't it be something if he was faking?"

"What?" she asked in surprise. She stared at Wallmann as if she expected him to sit up and start laughing.

"It was just a thought. I mean, what if he woke up and decided not to let us know?"

"Well, what are we supposed to do, pinch him every hour on the hour to see if he's faking?"

"Either that or put your gun to his head and cock it."

She frowned at him, as if trying to figure out whether he was kidding, and when he didn't say anything she took out her gun, touched the barrel to Wallmann's temple, and cocked it.

"Nothing," she said.

She was right, even though she had not been looking for the same things the Gunsmith had been looking for. Wallmann had not even twitched, and there was no doubt that he was totally unconscious.

"All right," he said, "put it away."

"How come you didn't do it?" she asked, holstering her gun.

"I don't take my gun out unless I'm going to use it."

"You have a lot of rules in your life, don't you?"

"Yes."

You probably have rules about getting involved with women, too, she thought, but she didn't voice it.

She walked to the window and said, "This window looks out onto the main street—such as it is."

"I know," he said, "I was out there, remember?"

"Oh yeah."

"Nervous?"

She turned to face him and said, "Yes. We're stuck in here, and who knows how many men Montalban can scare up to send against us?"

"We have one thing in our favor."

"What's that?"

"He thinks I'm alone," he said. "And another thing—he's going to think that I'm in my room with a woman."

"Me?"

"You."

"I wish we were," she said.

"So do I," he said.

THIRTY-FOUR

Although Pedro Montalban may not have been the smartest man in the world—or even in town—he *was* lucky. In this particular instance he was lucky because the room clerk in the hotel was his cousin.

"Here they come," Anne said. She was sitting by the window keeping watch, and spoke up when she saw Montalban and his friends—four of them—crossing the street and heading for the hotel.

Clint moved up behind her to peer out the window, and said, "They'll try my room first."

"You don't think they'll look for us right away after that?"

"Would you figure us to be up here in Wallmann's room with him?"

"No," she said, shaking her head.

"Then they'll regroup and try to figure out where I went with my woman."

"Then we still have time."

"We've got some time, yeah," Clint said. He turned to

look at Wallmann on the bed and said, "With any luck, something will happen up here soon."

Montalban's cousin was only too glad to give him Clint Adams's room number—in fact, he was too scared not to. Montalban signalled his men—Mantilla, Torres and two others who were hired for their guns—to follow him, and led the way down the hall to Clint's room. They all drew their guns, and Montalban gestured for one of them to kick the door in. Torres obeyed, and leaped into the room just before Montalban, who was followed by the others.

Confused, Montalban looked around the empty room, then turned and pushed past his men. He stalked angrily down the hall to the front desk and yanked his cousin up by grabbing a fistful of his shirtfront.

"Where did he go?" he demanded.

"Wha—?" his cousin said, eyes wide with fear. "I swear, cousin, I thought he was in his room with a girl."

"What girl?"

"An American woman."

"What did she look like?" Montalban asked. He did not know of any American women in town.

"Very good looking, cousin," the man said. "Red hair, a fine womanly shape—"

Montalban turned to his men, who had trickled out into the lobby behind him, and asked, "Has anyone seen such a woman?"

They all exchanged glances and shook their heads.

"How did they get past you?" Montalban demanded of his frightened cousin.

"They did not have to get past me," the man explained. "They could have gone out the back way—"

"Or," Montalban said, interrupting his cousin and

looking up toward the second floor, "gone upstairs. Do you have any empty rooms in the hotel?"

"About half of the rooms are empty."

Montalban released his hold on his cousin's shirt and said, "Then we will check them all."

"You do not have to do that," the clerk said.

Montalban stopped short and looked at his cousin.

"Why do you say that?"

"Because there is someone who can help you."

"Who?"

"The doctor."

"How can the doctor help me?"

"The girl went for him earlier and took him upstairs."

"To which room?" Montalban asked anxiously.

"I do not know. But he would."

"Yes," Montalban said, "he would. Thank you, cousin."

Montalban's gratitude was obvious, and the clerk felt that he had redeemed himself—and was relieved.

"I am leaving Torres outside the hotel in case they leave while we are gone. Once the doctor tells us what room they are in—and why they needed a doctor—we will be back."

"Yes, cousin."

"Andale," Montalban told the others, and they left to visit the doctor, leaving Pascal Torres behind.

"They're leaving," Anne said, bringing Clint back to the window.

He frowned and said, "How many went in?"

She thought a moment and then said, "Five." Then she realized why he'd asked, and added, "There's only four leaving."

"Right. One man was left behind, but we don't know if

he's inside or out."

Clint turned away from the window quickly, and Anne asked, "What are you going to do?"

"Since they've chosen to leave one man behind," Clint said, checking his modified Colt to make sure it was fully loaded, "we'd be foolish not to take advantage of their generosity."

"Are you going to kill him?"

"I'm going to take him out of the play," Clint said. "Wait here and wish me luck."

Clint took the back stairs down to the main level of the hotel, and then crept along the hall outside his room. He noticed that the door was open, and knew that Montalban had checked it already. Had he left to regroup, as he had suggested to Anne?

He moved farther down the hall until he was almost to the end, and then peered out. He saw a man standing by the front door and thought he recognized him as one of the men who had been in the saloon with Montalban.

There were a couple of ways to do this, but the most straightforward way seemed to be the best. He took his gun out, feeling justified in doing so, because if the man gave him any trouble, he'd surely use it.

Extending his arm, aiming the gun at the man by the door, he called out, "Hey, Señor!"

The man turned and froze at the sight of the gun.

"You understand English?" Clint asked.

"*Sî*—yes, Señor."

"Good. Drop your gun to the floor, friend." The man hesitated and Clint said, "Do me a favor and try something."

The man frowned, confused, and then lifted his gun

THE BOUNTY WOMEN

from its holster and dropped it to the floor.

"Good, now kick it out into the street."

The man obeyed and sent the revolver spinning out into the dust.

"Fine. Now walk this way. And you, behind the desk—"

The clerk stopped short and said, "Me, Señor?"

"Yeah, you. How'd Montalban know what room I was in? And don't lie to me."

"I told him, Señor."

"Why?"

"He is my cousin—and I am afraid of him."

"All right. Just stand still behind that counter, and I won't have any reason to kill you. Understand?"

"Oh yes, Señor."

"What's this fella's name?"

"Torres."

"All right, Torres, move toward me real slow. We're going for a walk."

"Sî, Señor."

Clint backed down the hall with Torres, leading the man to the open door of his room.

After a few moments Clint had the man hogtied to the bed, one appendage fastened to each bedpost, and he could see by the look on the man's face that he still expected to be killed.

"I'm not going to kill you," he said, then added, "unless you stick your head out of this room. If you do that, I will definitely kill you, even if I have to die doing it. Do you understand?"

"Sî, Señor."

"Very good. With a little luck, you'll be untied within a couple of hours."

Clint left the room and closed the door behind him. It remained ajar due to the broken lock, but did not swing open.

He went back to the front desk, where the clerk was still waiting, and asked, "Where did your cousin and his men go?"

"To see the doctor."

Clint didn't need to be told why, or who had told them about the doctor.

"I'm going upstairs for a minute," Clint said, "and I expect you still to be here when I come back."

"*Sí, Señor.*"

"Don't make me have to come looking for you."

"*No, Señor.*"

Clint went upstairs and let himself into Wallmann's room. Anne was standing by the window with her gun in her hand, and she breathed a sigh of relief when she saw him.

"What happened?" she asked.

"I can't explain, but when Montalban comes back, he's going to know where I am. He's not going to be sure whether or not I'm alone, though. He'll know there was a woman here, but he won't know that you can handle a gun."

"What are you going to do?"

"I'm going to wait for him downstairs and try to change his mind about Wallmann."

"You're going to face the four of them by yourself?"

"You'll be covering me from the window," he said. "If there's any shooting, feel free to open the window and join in—but don't do anything until I do. Understand?"

"I understand."

"With a little luck we'll resolve this right now," he said.

"Be careful."

"As careful as I can be. You too."

He gave her a little salute and then went downstairs to wait for Montalban and his men.

THIRTY-FIVE

When Pedro Montalban finished with Dr. Estrada, the good doctor had more of those cuts and bruises he had told Clint and Anne he'd been treating since he came to town—only these were his own.

Now that Montalban knew Wallmann's condition, he thought his job was going to be that much easier. Once he got past Clint Adams, he'd be home free. When he got to Wallmann's room, if the gunman wasn't already dead, he'd just put him out of his misery.

Now he had to figure out a way to cut Torres and Montilla out of the reward. They were his "partners," while the other two men were simply for hire.

"Pedro," Mantilla said.

"Si?" Pedro replied absently.

"Look."

Pedro looked ahead to where Montilla was pointing, and saw a man standing in front of the hotel. For a moment he thought it was Torres, but then he saw that it wasn't.

It was Adams.

"Remember," he told the other three men, "he's only one man with one gun."

He hoped the *gringo* would be fast enough to kill the other three before he, Montalban, killed him.

Clint recognized the man who had been in the saloon with Montalban and Torres, but knew instinctively that the other two men had been hired. Still, the first man he intended to plug, if push came to shove, was Montalban himself. The two gunmen had to be for hire, and if the man who was paying them fell, chances were they'd lose interest in the proceedings.

He hoped.

Anne Archer saw the four men walking toward the front of the hotel. Clint, who she knew was standing out there, was still out of her sight and she kept urging him mentally to move out where she could see him. She started to open the window so she could lean out for a look, but she suddenly became aware of movement behind her. She started to turn, but was too late as an iron grip took hold of her around the waist and throat . . .

"That's far enough, Montalban!" Clint called out. He moved out into the street so that Anne would be able to see him from the window.

"This is silly, *amigo*," Montalban called out. "We are fighting over a man who is already dead."

"He's not dead yet."

"He will be, my friend. As soon as we get by you, he will be as dead as you."

"You're making a mistake, Montalban. You and your men are taking on more than you can handle."

"You are one man, Señor," Montalban said. "No one man is a match for four."

"Think again," Clint said, with cold confidence in his tone.

"Pedro—" Mantilla said in a low voice.

"What?"

"What if he is right?"

"Nonsense."

"But who is he, Pedro, to think that he can be the match of four men? Wild Bill Hickok?"

"Hickok is dead," Montalban said, "and Wallmann is as good as dead. There is only one other man who could possibly . . ." He let his words trail off as he realized the implications of what he was saying.

"Pedro? Who do you mean?"

"It cannot be," Montalban said, trying to convince himself. "What are the odds against two such men being in the same town at the same time?"

"What men?" Torres demanded hoarsely.

"Bill Wallmann," Montalban said, "and . . . the Gunsmith."

Clint sensed that the resolve of the four men might be wavering, and decided to apply some pressure.

"Come on, Montalban. If we're going to do this thing, let's get it done."

"Pedro," Mantilla said, "is he the Gunsmith?"

"It does not matter," Montalban insisted. "There is too much money at stake."

"But perhaps we should—"

"I am going to pull my gun out. I suggest the rest of you do the same. It is the only chance you have."

"Pedro, wait—" Mantilla said, but even as he did he saw Montalban pull his gun free of his holster. In a panic he tried to get his out also.

Clint saw what Montalban was doing, even as his own hand was streaking for his weapon. Montalban had drawn his gun and then suddenly *ducked behind* the other three men! The Gunsmith wasn't about to let that stop him, though. The other men were drawing their guns, so he was justified in doing what he did.

He killed Mantilla first, then rapidly pulled the trigger of his modified, double-action Colt, plugging the other two before they could reach their guns.

Montalban was suddenly out in the open—and the transition was too swift for him to comprehend. His reaction was instinctive, even as his mind swirled with confusion. His gun, already in his hand, began to come up and Clint fired once. The bullet caught Montalban in the chest and drove him back a step or two before he fell to the ground with his associates.

It was then that Clint realized something was wrong. No shots had come from the hotel window, and when he looked up he saw that it was not open, nor was Anne visible. He knew what had happened even before it was verified by the man's appearance at the hotel entrance.

It was Bill Wallmann.

"Haven't seen you since that logging town, Adams," Wallmann said. "What brings you here?"

"Bill, listen to me. You're not well—"

"Is that a fact?"

"What just happened a few moments ago?"

"What are you talking—"

"Humor me."

"I woke up. Found somebody in my room, too. A woman."

"Is she—"

THE BOUNTY WOMEN

"She's fine. She's tied up on the bed. She was with Sandy Spillane when she tried to take me in. Are you here to take me back, Clint?"

"What day is this, Bill?"

"I don't see—"

"What day?"

"It's Tuesday."

"No, it's not, Bill," Clint corrected him. "Today's Thursday."

"Can't be," Wallmann said, frowning.

"You weren't sleeping, Bill. You were unconscious. The doctor here said that you have some pressure on your brain. He said you could either wake up or die."

Suddenly Wallmann's left hand went to his temple, and pressed there.

"I've been getting these headaches . . ." he said.

"You see? You need help, Bill, medical attention. Let me take you—"

"You mean," Wallmann went on, as if he hadn't heard Clint, "I lost two days, just like that?"

"And could have very easily lost your life. Let me help you."

Wallmann stared into space for a few moments, and Clint realized that he probably could have drawn and fired in that time, but the opportunity was gone as quickly as it had come.

"All right," Wallmann said finally. "You can help me."

"Good," Clint said, but he watched in confusion as Wallmann stepped out into the street and then turned to face him.

"I'm going to kill you, Clint."

"What? But you just said—"

"I'm going to kill you unless you kill me."

In a flash, Clint knew what Wallmann had in mind.

"This isn't the way, Bill—"

"You can tell me that, Clint? How would you rather die? From a bullet, or from something unknown inside your head?"

"It doesn't have to be unknown—"

"I ain't gonna let no doctors cut me."

"Bill—"

"Forget it, Adams!" Wallmann snapped. "At least this way I'll have a question answered that I've been wondering about for a long time. Who's better, you or me?"

"Dammit, Bill, don't make me—"

"Now, Gunsmith!" Wallmann said, and his right hand sped toward his gun.

Damn, but he was fast! Probably the fastest the Gunsmith had ever faced. Clint drew and pulled the trigger on his gun, and as his shot flew toward Wallmann, he heard Wallmann's gun speak. No one had ever matched his shot before!

As he watched his bullet strike Wallmann dead center in the chest, he felt the other man's bullet tug at the fabric of his left shirtsleeve.

His heart was pounding, because if any man had ever had a chance of beating him, it was Wallmann, only Clint was convinced that the man had rushed his shot. He was also convinced that Wallmann had tried his best to kill him, because his pride wouldn't have let him do otherwise.

And he'd come damn close—closer than the Gunsmith liked to think about.

He looked at his arm and saw blood beginning to stain the shirt, but it was just a scratch. He walked over to

Wallmann, hoping for a chance to talk to the man before he died, but there was no chance.

Bill Wallmann was dead.

THIRTY-SIX

Anne was tied up on the bed, just as Wallmann had said she was, and by the time Clint had her cut free, the local law was there, looking for explanations. Anne helped out by producing the poster on Wallmann, and the sheriff, looking for the easiest way out, accepted that there had been a gun battle for the right to face Wallmann, and Clint had won all around.

As Clint tightened the ropes that were holding Wallmann's body securely to his own saddle, Anne asked, "How far will you come back with me?"

"Just over the border," he said. "First town we come to, you'll just have to show the sheriff the poster and he'll get you your money."

"And after that?"

"Anne—"

"No, never mind, Clint," she said, looking down at him from astride her horse. "I know what happens after that."

Clint didn't say anything; he just climbed up on Duke's back and led the way to the border.

"Hold up!" a man's voice called out, just as they were about to cross the river.

Clint pulled Duke to a stop and turned to see who was calling.

"Who is it?" Anne asked.

"Jake Benteen."

"Wasn't he looking for Wallmann too?"

"Yep," Clint said, as Benteen started riding toward them, "he sure was."

"What's he going to—?"

"Just sit tight."

When Benteen caught up with them he dismounted, lifted a corner of the tarpaulin that covered Wallmann's body, and took a good look at his face. Nodding, he turned and faced Clint.

"I thought you said you weren't hunting him?"

"I wasn't," Clint said, "but the lady was."

"Anne Archer, Mr. Benteen," Anne said, introducing herself. "We're in the same business."

"So I heard."

Anne watched Benteen, holding her breath, waiting for the man to make his move. Was he going to try to take Wallmann from them?

Clint had no such thoughts.

"Looks like you beat me to him, miss," Benteen said. "Mind if I ride a ways with you folks? I'm kind of anxious to get back home. Clint?"

Clint looked at Anne, then said to Benteen. "You're welcome to ride with us, Jake."

"Much obliged."

As they approached the river, Jake leaned over and asked, "You take him, Clint?"

"Yes," Clint said. "I promised to help her, and that's what I did."

"Was he as fast as they say?"

"Faster."

"Well," Benteen said, "I guess it was better that you got to him before I did, then."

"Better for him," Clint said. If anyone else had found him—even Jake Benteen—Clint felt that Wallmann would still be alive . . . and that just wasn't what Bill Wallmann had wanted. He'd decided that it was time to die the way he'd lived, by the gun.

A man had that right.

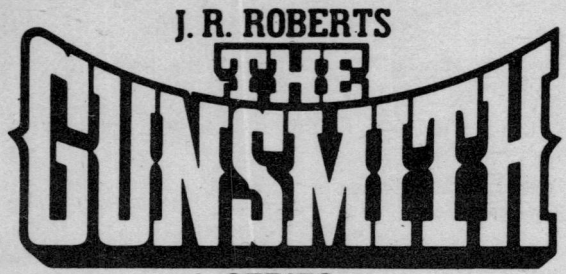

J. R. ROBERTS
THE GUNSMITH
SERIES

☐ 30928-3	THE GUNSMITH	#1: MACKLIN'S WOMEN	$2.50
☐ 30878-3	THE GUNSMITH	#2: THE CHINESE GUNMEN	$2.50
☐ 30858-9	THE GUNSMITH	#3: THE WOMAN HUNT	$2.25
☐ 30925-9	THE GUNSMITH	#5: THREE GUNS FOR GLORY	$2.50
☐ 30861-9	THE GUNSMITH	#6: LEADTOWN	$2.25
☐ 30862-7	THE GUNSMITH	#7: THE LONGHORN WAR	$2.25
☐ 30901-1	THE GUNSMITH	#8: QUANAH'S REVENGE	$2.50
☐ 30923-2	THE GUNSMITH	#9: HEAVYWEIGHT GUN	$2.50
☐ 30924-0	THE GUNSMITH	#10: NEW ORLEANS FIRE	$2.50
☐ 30931-3	THE GUNSMITH	#11: ONE-HANDED GUN	$2.50
☐ 30926-7	THE GUNSMITH	#12: THE CANADIAN PAYROLL	$2.50
☐ 30927-5	THE GUNSMITH	#13: DRAW TO AN INSIDE DEATH	$2.50
☐ 30922-4	THE GUNSMITH	#14: DEAD MAN'S HAND	$2.50
☐ 30905-4	THE GUNSMITH	#15: BANDIT GOLD	$2.50
☐ 30886-4	THE GUNSMITH	#16: BUCKSKINS AND SIX-GUNS	$2.25
☐ 30907-0	THE GUNSMITH	#17: SILVER WAR	$2.50
☐ 30908-9	THE GUNSMITH	#18: HIGH NOON AT LANCASTER	$2.50
☐ 30909-7	THE GUNSMITH	#19: BANDIDO BLOOD	$2.50

Prices may be slightly higher in Canada.

Available at your local bookstore or return this form to:

CHARTER BOOKS
Book Mailing Service
P.O. Box 690, Rockville Centre, NY 11571

Please send me the titles checked above. I enclose _____. Include 75¢ for postage and handling if one book is ordered; 25¢ per book for two or more not to exceed $1.75. California, Illinois, New York and Tennessee residents please add sales tax.

NAME _____

ADDRESS _____

CITY _____ STATE/ZIP _____

(allow six weeks for delivery.)

A1